A face, an expres
glass window of h
on his memory. Pallid features, devoid of emotion yet ruthless in their own way, staring at him out of the crowd, able to penetrate the one-way glass. Seeing him, and hating him. Which was impossible, he had told himself that a thousand times as he had tossed restlessly in his bed last night. A spectre that haunted him, an invincible being that could pass through armed guards as easily as it could see him in his car. Lying there in the darkness, cringing from the shadows that took shape and moved: came close, darted away before he could identify them.

There were voices, too, indiscernible hate-filled, threatening whispers, mocking him because of his terror. Once his thick fingers had groped for the alarm bell but he had snatched them away just as they touched it.

'Is something wrong, Premier?' Orobin would have grunted from the open doorway, his hand resting habitually on an empty holster inside his jacket.

'Yes, Comrade, the darkness, the shadows, they frighten me. Switch on the light and stay with me until daylight.'

THE BLACK FEDORA

Guy N. Smith

THE SHERIDAN
BOOK COMPANY

This edition published in 1994 by
The Sheridan Book Company

First published in Great Britain by Sphere Books Ltd 1991

Typeset in Baskerville by
Fleet Graphics, Enfield, Middlesex
Printed and bound in Great Britain by
Cox & Wyman Ltd, Reading, Berkshire

ISBN 1-85501-515-3

For Boz & Jeannette, and for Martin
who wore the black fedora

Many arrows, loosed several ways,
Come to one mark.

William Shakespeare

CHAPTER ONE

The man in the black fedora joined the peace convoy five miles east of Salisbury Plain.

The late June day was unprecedentedly hot, the rain and gales of the past few weeks akin to an uneasy dream which was receding with waking. By mid-day the puddles on the sides of the busy A303 had almost evaporated; by tomorrow the mud would begin to bake and crack. The area of high pressure which had been static over the Atlantic for a week had finally eased its way across the British Isles, and the weather forecasters were cautiously predicting that it would remain there for the next few days, possibly over the weekend. The motoring organizations were right with their forecasts also, and the traffic queues had begun to build up in earnest.

The five-mile jam on the main road was caused by a combination of a police roadblock and a dozen or so dilapidated, unroadworthy, unlicensed buses and vans of varying makes and sizes, each daubed with psychedelic aerosol slogans that varied between police insults and an idealistic society brought about by unilateral nuclear disarmament. These vehicles were the remnants of the mighty raggle-taggle convoy that had clashed with the law a mile outside Stonehenge on the previous day, the mechanically wounded with their boiling radiators and empty petrol tanks, all of which would be rectified at the taxpayers' expense in order to trundle them on their way. Get them out of the county, over the border into Gloucestershire, and forget them. Pass the buck.

Breakdown trucks with flashing amber lights were adding to the chaos; the situation had to get worse before it got better. The stifling atmosphere was heavy with the stench of petrol as overall-clad men, supervised by police, poured fuel into the yellow double-decker at the head of the unsightly queue. A uniformed officer motioned to a watching youth to stand back; tobacco or cannabis, it mattered not, the smouldering cigarette presented a far greater immediate threat.

Further down the road a group of hippies had a fire going on the grass verge, were attempting to cook something over the flames. Another means of protest rather than a genuine desire to heat food. They would move on when they were ready, and not until. But overall, the taciturn inspector in the parked patrol car congratulated himself, the operation had been a success. A show of force with no more than minor skirmishes, and the annual summer solstice pilgrimage had been turned back. By nightfall it would all be over, tomorrow a lengthy report would be submitted to the chief constable, filed and forgotten. Until next June. Mentally he found himself urging his men to hurry up and get this scum over the county border. Because it was too damned hot to sit around here.

It was five o'clock in the afternoon before the convoy was trundling its way north-east, its progress marked by a cloud of exhaust fumes that was slow to disperse in the windless atmosphere. And the man in the black fedora was sleeping peacefully on the top deck of the lead bus, an uninvited passenger who, so far, had gone unchallenged. Nobody had asked his name, so he had not told them. It was the unwritten law of the open road, and in these times of police harassment there was strength in numbers. The travellers needed this stranger as much as he needed them. He was welcome.

'Who's the new guy?' Benjamin had climbed to the status of leader of the hippies over the last six months. A gradual process that had begun with his acquisition of the bus from the breaker's yard and a combination of mechanical knowledge which had rendered it basically mobile. He owned a means of transport and the others were happy to go along with him for that reason. In his mid-twenties he was a formidable figure, over six feet tall in his ragged slipper socks, his muscular frame threatening to burst out of his tattered, unwashed clothing. His beard grew wild, straggled, a matted mane spotted with particles of spilled food. One who combined education with primitive living, his unkemptness a deliberate tilt at society.

'Which guy?' The petite, dark haired girl dozing beside the driver's seat stirred, yawned. In spite of her stained jeans and grubby T-shirt, there was a degree of self-respect about her which one noted if one looked hard enough. In keeping with the rest of them, but somehow different. A hanger-on who had become caught up with the nomads, went with them possibly because she had nowhere else to go. A victim of modern day circumstances, A-levels, or even a degree, which ultimately had proved useless. Or simply because her man had opted for that lifestyle. She had been almost asleep, momentarily she resented her lover's interruption. Instinctively she brushed back a strand of hair, a further sign that she did not altogether neglect her appearance. Her skin was smooth, because she washed.

'Ferret face, the one that looks like an out of work undertaker's assistant.' Benjamin glanced in his wing mirror, saw that the battered green ambulance behind had pulled on to the verge; another break-down. Well, Midge could sort out his own problems, catch them up if ever he got that heap of scrap going again. If not, then that was *his* hard luck. They had wated enough time already.

'I've no idea,' Penny shifted her position, her sweat-soaked clothing clinging damply to her slim body. 'Just like I've no idea who the other fifteen on this bus are. They come and go. Why?'

'Just curious,' Benjamin changed up a gear, felt the clutch shudder and hoped it would hold out for the next hundred miles or so. 'He's some kind of weirdo, not one of us.'

'You haven't even spoken to him,' there was a mild reprimand in her tone, an instinctive support for the homeless itinerant.

'No, but he gives me the creeps. Deadpan faces and funereal clothes don't mix. Not in this set-up, anyway.'

'It's probably just an image he's trying to create,' she yawned again, stretched her legs, felt the knee of her old denims rip another half inch. 'If he doesn't play to the rules, you can always chuck him off, Benjie.'

'Oh, sure,' the driver leaned back in his seat. 'No problem there. But one has to be careful.'

'A *pig*?'

'It's always a possibility, but they wouldn't have any need to plant a mole. They know where we're going, where we've been. They could have searched us, taken every vehicle off the road, thrown the whole goddamned book at us. But they won't do that because it wouldn't serve any purpose. Fine us, and we don't have any money to pay. All the jails are over-crowded so they won't lock us up. They just want to get us over the border into the next county. "Keep 'em on the move" is their motto, same as it's always been. Maybe it was stupid to try for Stonehenge again, everybody knew we wouldn't get through. A kind of protest, really, but it's getting boring every year. Next time we'll give it a miss. They'll be waiting to move us on from the Cantlin Stone. The Chase, too. All along, we're on a loser. There are just the odd places where they tolerate us, ghettos really.'

'Like me, you're getting pissed off.' There was resignation as well as tiredness in her tone. Opting out of society was damned hard work, a bloody sight harder than conforming. In the end the System would wear you down, whip you into submission.

'It's been fun,' he laughed and it sounded strained. 'All the same, I'd like to know more about that feller in black.'

It took the small convoy three days to reach the Cantlin Stone on the Welsh borderlands, a meandering route that by-passed Gloucester and Hereford. Three of the vehicles had dropped out, broken down or gone their separate ways. Benjamin didn't know for sure which, only that they weren't there when the others pulled in for their overnight stops. Maybe Midge hadn't managed to get the ambulance going again.

The Cantlin Stone was a wild place set in the foothills, an expanse of moorland which they had visited for the past three years. This year they were early; too early for the Magic Mushroom Festival, an event which had assumed notoriety, thanks to the media. Just because the hallucinatory fungi grew here in abundance the newspapers billed it as a site for drug orgies whilst, in fact, the mushrooms played only a small part in the annual gathering. The site was secluded. Left alone, you could drop out of society forever except that the surrounding hill farmers regarded it as their domain even though it was, in fact, common land. Petitions had led to an injunction being granted in the high court five years ago, and since then the place had become another Stonehenge, with barriers and a police presence. Usually the hippies were left alone for a few days before being moved on. The annual pilgrimage had become a period of brief nostalgia now, nothing more. Memories of how it had once been and never would be again, then you carried on your way to wherever. Always on the move.

But, Benjamin thought, they might just have forestalled the law this year by being early; it wasn't mushroom time, there would be fewer than twenty vehicles on the common at the most. The pigs *might* even turn a blind eye to them. Which seemed to be the case when he pulled the shuddering bus off the road into the shade of a spruce plantation. There wasn't a cop in sight. Yet.

'How long are we stopping here?' Penny stayed behind in her seat after the others had disembarked.

'Till after the Solstice.' Benjamin wiped the sweat from his grimed features, sat staring at the sunset with a kind of reverence in his expression. 'But that'll depend on the fuzz.' The fine weather would continue, he didn't need the radio to tell him that. 'We're early. We have a fortnight to kill, we daren't risk the Chase before then.' There was a tenseness about him now, a single-mindedness that had his eyes slitting beneath the bushy brows. 'If we get moved off the Chase then there's no place close enough to Lichfield to go, and the Festival doesn't start until 9 July.

Add another week on to that and we've got a lot of time to play with. Time we don't want, and all these other bums tagging along don't help.'

'Couldn't we just move off after dark and leave them here?'

'Could do. Maybe we will, nearer the time. But the chances are they'd only follow us on to the Chase. Seven Springs is the obvious step from here. On the other hand, we need the bastards. Moving on a convoy is a lot more difficult than just telling Benjie's Bus to get the hell out of anywhere. On our own we'd stand out like a sore thumb.'

'I don't like it, Benjie.' It was the first time that Penny had voiced her unease, an anxiety that bordered on fear. 'It's out of our league, it's going too far.'

'If you want to drop out, go ahead. But go *now*!' His dark eyes narrowed, seemed to burn into her.

'I didn't say that,' her lower lip trembled. There were times when she was scared of her lover and this was one of them. Benjamin's uncontrollable rages were unpredictable. One minute he was slow and easy going, the next he resembled an infuriated grizzly bear. You could never be sure of him, not even when you were the closest to him that anybody had ever been. A mixture of gentleness and violence, one misinterpreted word was enough to trigger him off. You never really knew what he was thinking and that was very frightening.

'All right,' he shrugged, forced a smile. 'You know why we're here, where we're going, and what we have to do. I haven't changed my mind. Like I said, all this running around has been marking time, a roundabout way of getting where you want to go so that you can do what you have to do. It won't be easy, we have to bide our time, wait our chance. But such an opportunity won't present itself again. It's all or bust, like an eclipse that happens once in every fifty years. If you don't see it then, you never will. We bide our time, play our cards. There won't be a second chance.'

'I'll start some food.' She stood up, told herself that the weakness in her legs was due to the long ride. Her temples were pounding, that was due to the heat, as would be the migraine that she would surely suffer before morning.

Benjamin had offered her the chance to opt out and she had spurned it. As he had said, there would not be a second chance.

Penny cooked a lentil and bean stew over a fire which the others had made from deadwood gathered out of the conifer thicket. They clustered round, brought their own plates and spoons, their expressions eager in the flickering firelight, companions in transit. Nothing mattered except today; trails had crossed and might part tomorrow. Names did not matter, you remembered a meeting, a face. You might meet again one day. The food, the fire, were communal; you paid your share of the fuel for the vehicles, the more who travelled, the cheaper it was.

Penny surreptitiously eyed the stranger sitting cross-legged just beyond the fireglow. A loner, most of them were that, but this one did not fit the mould. The fedora was pulled low over his forehead as if he consciously sought to hide his lean features in its shadow; if she had not seen them earlier it would have been impossible to discern them now. High cheekbones which gave the impression of stretching the pallid skin, pale blue eyes that flicked from side to side, missed nothing. It was difficult to imagine those thin lips ever smiling. Deadpan, as Benjamin had said. The stranger was maybe 5 foot 9 inches tall, his lithe body reminding one of a coiled spring, sombre in those black Levis with a matching shirt.

Penny shivered in spite of the warmth from the fire. Benjamin had summed the other up aptly, a mortician's assistant. The newcomer was maybe twenty-five, possibly older; older than any of them around this campfire. If his clothing had been torn, streaked with filth, then he would have aroused little interest. But it wasn't, just a film of road dust, the hallmark of the traveller. And there was something else about him which she could not figure out right now, something that was . . . *frightening*.

'Man, what's your name?' Benjamin pushed forward out of the throng, knelt in front of the black-clad figure, the hippy leader's pose arrogant, threatening.

The other looked up, his eyes meeting those of the red-bearded man, seeming to glint like chips of blue ice in the firelight. Relaxed yet poised, meeting arrogance with defiance. Slowly he spooned stew into his mouth, swallowed before asking in a voice that was cultured and gentle, yet seemed to vibrate the still night air, 'Why?'

'Because I asked, that's why!' Benjamin's thick fingers flexed, clenched.

The stranger took his time, adjusted his hat before he spoke, and when he did his voice was so low that the listeners had to strain to catch the single word.

'Haggard.'

'Haggard?' The leader dwelt on the name as though seeking some significance in it. 'Haggard . . . what?'

'Just Haggard. What's yours?'

Only on a handful of previous occasions had Penny seen her lover taken aback. His Adam's apple bobbed as he struggled to speak, attempted to retrieve his composure. 'Benjamin,' he replied, and added, '*just* Benjamin.' It was like an admission of guilt, a confession that had been wrested from him.

'Pleased to know you, Benjamin.' The man called Haggard scraped out his bowl, set it down on the ground. 'Now we know each other, if that's what you were after.'

'You wear that hat in bed . . . Haggard?' Benjamin was suddenly aggressive again, attempting to regain any ground, any face, which he might have lost in front of his followers, his girl.

'Sometimes,' Haggard regarding him unsmiling, unblinking. 'Depends where I sleep, whether it's winter or summer. You got any objection to it?'

'No.' The big man licked his lips, pursed them. 'No, I've got no objection, but this happens to be my bus and I reckon I've a right to know who's travelling on it. You going anywhere special?'

'Not really,' Haggard leaned back against the trunk of a spruce tree, folded his arms. 'Just on the move. Like you. I'd be glad to travel with you anywhere you're going. If I don't like it, I can always get off. Is that all right with you?'

Benjamin nodded slowly, then, without another word, he stood up, turned and walked back towards the bus. And that was when Penny's skin goose-pimpled and she found herself looking away from the man who wore a black fedora and called himself Haggard, suddenly hoping that he had not noticed her watching him, and that to him she was just one of the fireside crowd and not Benjamin's girl.

Because she knew, without any doubt, that this stranger was dangerous. And the most terrifying thing of all was that she did not know why.

CHAPTER TWO

There were only two people in whose presence Chief Superintendent Clive Gardener of the Lichfield police felt uncomfortable. One was the chief constable, the other was the bishop.

Gardener, a taciturn man with thin greying hair and a stone and a half overweight, had come straight from a meeting with the chief. A briefing, in fact, nothing more, but in spite of his size and rank, the superintendent had been made to feel decidedly inferior. 'Yes, sir', when you really meant 'no, sir', and a low alcohol lager from the cocktail cabinet which you were supposed to sip with relish in support of the drink-driving campaign, even though the beer tasted like the residue from a squeezed-out dishcloth. You were invited to express your own opinions, had them instantly quashed with reasons that sounded logical until you thought about them afterwards.

'I've made arrangements for you to have a meeting with the bishop at two-thirty this afternoon, Chief Superintendent,' a vestige of a smile that said, 'and don't you be a second late.' 'I think it is imperative that we liaise with the Church over security arrangements for those vital few days. Of course, you will only be offering *advice*, in no way must we be seen to be dictating. You understand that, don't you?' Another condescending smile that had Gardener shifting uneasily in his chair.

'Yes, sir,' yet again. Gardener drained his glass. It seemed to leave a sour coating on his palate. For God's sake, don't pour me another.

'Very well, then, it would seem that this whole business is centred on the cathedral during the finale of the Festival. That doesn't mean that we can relax our vigilance from the very commencement of the Festival, though.'

'We', of course, meaning 'you', Gardener reflected wryly as he drove back down the A51 towards Lichfield. He would delegate, as he was supposed to, but if anything went wrong then it was his backside that would be well and firmly kicked with a top level boot. It's quite simple really, Gardener, all you have to do is protect an unwelcome foreign dignitary as well as the Lichfield Gospels. The former is under threat of assassination, the latter might be defaced or stolen. By people with totally unrelated motives. The Festival just happens to be the focal point for both parties. And, to enrich the mixture, we have a peace convoy camped on the Chase whom we currently have neither the manpower nor the authority to evict. That we shall attend to after the Festival, by which time the hippies will probably have moved on, anyway. Get your priorities right. Not that we think you can't handle these matters, Chief Superintendent, in addition to policing the Festival crowds, but we have been assigned a special duties officer from Scotland Yard. Detective-Inspector Walters will be answerable directly to the assistant commissioner. So don't get trying to tell him his job.

Gardener stopped off at the Angel Croft for lunch; there wasn't time to go home and at least he was on the doorstep of his next assignment. Two minutes' walk, less if he hurried; he kept glancing at his watch, ordered a second orange juice in the hope that it would remove the taste of that lager. Low alcohol drinks gave off the same fumes as the real McCoy, and beery breath might not go down well with the bishop.

Gardener left the hotel at 2.25. Promptness was a virtue upon which he prided himself. An early arrival was as bad as being late. Worse, in fact. It immediately put you at a disadvantage because your host could keep you waiting, and waiting was all part of the demoralizing process. The policeman played it himself, deliberately kept a lower ranking officer fidgeting outside in the waiting room. By the time you saw him, his nervousness was at a peak. The old schoolmaster's trick with erring pupils, a ploy that had them confessing their misdemeanours simply to get it over and done with. Well, the chief superintendent wasn't going to put himself at the bishop's mercy that easily.

All the same, Clive Gardener was kept waiting until 2.40. Thank God that the bishop did not reside in the Palace these days; it had been turned over to a preparatory school some years ago, the holy man electing for the comfort and economy of an ordinary house in the Close. The Palace would have been just too awesome to contemplate today.

'Ah, Chief Superintendent, how good of you to spare the time to come and see me.' The bishop was tall, almost skeletal, but his narrow features gave an impression of saintliness rather than austerity. There was a genuineness about the clasp of those bony fingers, a smile that was the epitome of sincerity. 'I must say that I find it rather flattering to have the eyes of the political world focussed on our city at the time of the Festival.'

Damn it, I never looked up how to address a bishop. Gardener's stomach muscles tightened as he lowered himself into the chair opposite the ornate desk. Slip-up number one, he had failed for once in his usual fastidious attention to detail.

'A situation that is worrying the police as well as the Church, Bishop,' it *sounded* all right, more respectful than 'sir'. He breathed a little easier. 'But it was bound to happen. I mean, relations with Poland have improved, our own prime minister has visited that country. Jaruzelski himself has been to Britain. Now he is sending his premier. I think it might have been preferable had the general come again himself, the press have dug up a lot of unsavoury facts about this fellow Kosminski, doubtless most of them fabricated to sell sensational tabloids.' Gardener checked himself, a policeman was not supposed to voice personal opinions. It was just that the bishop exuded an air of confidentiality which became infectious.

'I see, Chief Superintendent,' the bishop leaned forward, his voice almost a whisper, 'that you have done your homework on this man.'

Testing me out, Gardener thought, or else wanting me to put into words what he doesn't want to go on record as having said. 'Much of it is rumour, Bishop. Unfounded facts, malicious gossip and supposition that have created an atmosphere of hostility. In 1889 there was a Pole by the same name who was committed to a British asylum, purported by some to be Jack the Ripper. They say that the Polish premier is a descendant of this man. Folklore, a legend created to stir up international hatred towards Premier Kosminksi. They also claim that Kosminski's uncle was a Nazi who is buried in the Commonwealth Cemetery on the Chase. I've personally checked the names on the German graves there and I can't find a Kosminski. But that doesn't mean a thing, it could have been an uncle on his mother's side. Personally, I treat these stories with scepticism. But we can't get away from the fact that Kosminski was instrumental in the Gdansk shootings . . . and there are an awful lot of naturalized Poles in this area! Add that to the memories of the Katyn massacre of 14,000 Polish soldiers, which many still believe to have been perpetrated by the Nazis in 1940, although we now know that the Russians were the culprits, and if Kosminski's uncle *was* a Nazi then we've got a potential cauldron of trouble liable to come to the boil. We can't rule out an assassination attempt.'

'You mean . . . you've had a . . . tip-off?' There was sudden concern on the bishop's angular features, a pursing of the thin, bloodless lips, and the long fingers stroking the pointed jaw trembled slightly.

'Not directly, Bishop. Again, rumours, unfounded like the rest. But Kosminski's life is in danger, we have to accept that, and it would be easier to assassinate him on British soil than it would be on Polish.'

'I see,' the other relaxed slightly, then said, 'but the Lichfield Gospels are under threat, you know that. That anonymous letter last week, I spoke to your detective-inspector about it. Some animal rights group, he thought . . .'

Gardener nodded, he had to accept that the bishop's priorities were different from his own; centuries old vellum sheets were more important to the Church than an international crisis. 'These animal libbers are crazy, there's no knowing what lengths they will go to for the most trivial of reasons. The St Chad Gospels have been around since the eighth century and now somebody is threatening to destroy them because each page of vellum takes one whole animal skin to make. But, of course, we are not overlooking the possibility that an attempt might be made either to deface or to steal them.'

'Their worth is estimated in millions of pounds, not to mention their value to this cathedral!' The bishop entwined his fingers in despair as he allowed himself to contemplate the worst. 'But they could never be sold, they are as easily recognizable as the Mappa Mundi. No, Chief Superintendent, I think we can rule out theft.'

'I'm afraid not, Bishop,' the policeman averted his eyes – disagreeing with the bishop was almost as nerve-racking as presenting a conflicting opinion to the chief constable. 'A ruthless private collector, a millionaire crook, for want of a better term, would be more than happy to have them adorning the walls of his illicit Aladdin's Cave, believe you me. We have a file of such men, supplied by Interpol, but these chaps are cunning. They don't keep masterpieces in their attics, they have their own secret museums. Priceless antiques are bought and sold without ever seeing daylight. This is the reason why a police guard will be mounted on the Lichfield Gospels throughout the Festival, Bishop. It's not the animal rights activists who worry us, they're small fry. It's the master criminals. But you could make life easier for us all, Bishop, if you would have the facsimiles on show and the originals under lock and key. That way, none of us would have so much to lose.' Gardener tensed, held his breath; he had said what he had come here to say, got it out of his system and off his conscience. But the final say remained with the other.

'No, no!' There was a note of irritation, stubbornness, in the bishop's tone. 'People come from all over the world to gaze upon the Gospels. Pilgrims. It would be deceiving them, cheating them. Some time ago we lent the Gospels to Aberystwyth, part of them are Welsh, you know. They were on public display there, quite safe, just as they have been, and still are, in our own cathedral here. I will not hide them, Chief Superintendent!' Anger now, the veins on his wrinkled neck corded as it was thrust forward in a show of defiance that bordered on petulance.

'All right,' Gardener was not going to argue, leave that to the chief constable. 'But we can only supply a guard throughout the Festival. The chief constable has instructed me accordingly.' So blame him, not me. 'Our concern is that there is a peace convoy camped within a dozen miles of here, a ragbag circus of anti-everything that society has accepted for centuries. We fear that an attempt to destroy or deface the Gospels could come from there. But not theft. If there's a plot to steal them it'll be from somebody much more sophisticated. Professionals, probably an international gang.'

The bishop was clearly worried, drumming his fingers on the mahogany desktop, closing his eyes briefly. Perhaps praying, Gardener thought, and he found the idea strangely disturbing. The silence was awkward, embarrassing, lasting for perhaps half a minute until those grey eyes flickered open and regarded him steadily. And when the bishop spoke his voice was hoarse, a cracked whisper in which there was no mistaking the inner fear that plagued him.

'Chief Superintendent,' the fingers had ceased drumming, were clenched so that the knuckles showed white, 'do you . . . do you believe in . . . *Satan*?'

Gardener's mouth opened but no words came. He didn't know whether to nod or to shake his head. Yea or nay. He believed in evil, he came into contact with it daily. But a horned bogeyman with cloven hooves rising up out of hell's fires? 'I . . . I . . . '

'Not as a being, perhaps,' the bishop came to his rescue, 'rather as an evil that is amongst us daily. Just as God is with us. Which is what I believed, and still do. And yet, Superintendent, if I told you that the Antichrist is supposedly coming in person to our holy city then you would doubtless, and quite rightly, think that my senses had deserted me, would you not?'

Again Gardener stared, afraid to speak, not knowing what to say. The room seemed to tilt, his vision blurred for a second. His mouth was dry and he was aware of the cloying taste of that low alcohol lager which he had drunk earlier.

'I think I should mention it.' The Bishop tried to smile but his lips quivered and his words shook. 'The dean had an anonymous phone call this morning. A man who spoke with a foreign accent. The caller said that the Festival was the time for the coming of the Antichrist, that he would manifest himself to us, that evil would triumph and God would be destroyed in a day. Just that. Then, whoever it was, rang off.'

'A nutter,' Gardener mused, his sigh sounded like a deflating Christmas balloon. 'We get them all the time. When there's a murder we can expect up to a dozen telephoned confessions. We don't have a hope in . . . there's no chance of being able to trace the caller, Bishop. Our priority is to protect both the Gospels and the Polish premier. But I'll bear that phone call in mind. If you get any more, let us know.' Because we won't be able to do a damned thing about them either.

'Thank you.' There was relief in the other's expression now, as though he had been brooding on the terrible prospect of the Antichrist all morning. Now he had reported the matter to the police, done his duty however ridiculous it seemed. 'I'm relying on you, Chief Superintendent . . . '

'We'll do our best, Bishop.' Gardener felt it was

time this meeting was brought to a close, a kind of gentle winding down to the point of departure. 'But we shall need to know the cathedral's role in the Festival proceedings right down to the smallest detail.'

'I will supply you with a programme of events. There will be an opening service, of course. And then there's the big finale. In past years it has been a firework display alongside Stowe Pool, but this time it is something more spectacular. We plan to stage a mock siege of the cathedral by the Roundheads. I believe the Sealed Knot are supervising that part of it. In any case, I will arrange for you to have any information you need.'

'Thank you, Bishop. Doubtless the Polish premier will be the guest of honour at this mock battle and that's another headache for us. I understand that he has also requested a visit to both the Commonwealth Cemetery and the Katyn Memorial on Cannock Chase, both of which create potentially explosive situations.'

'You *will* guard the Lichfield Gospels carefully, won't you, Chief Superintendent?' Almost a plea, a holy man concerned for the safety of his saintly exhibits, the visit of a communist premier a mere triviality by comparison. And secretly fearful lest the Antichrist might manifest himself, a lurking childhood terror rekindled.

'We shall do everything within our power, Bishop.' Clive Gardener rose to his feet, saw by the clock on the oak panelling that it was 3.45. An hour had seemed an eternity.

Outside he stood gazing at the cathedral almost reverently. He experienced a fleeting sense of humility in which being a top policeman counted for nothing. A towering structure of great beauty with its triple spires, a place of worship that had witnessed violence and bloodshed over the centuries and might well do so again. And, above all, he felt over-awed by the responsibility which had been bestowed upon him. International intrigue did not come to places like Lichfield, it was reserved for the capitals of the world. At least, he tried to convince himself of that. And failed.

It was four o'clock when he entered his office. The intercom on his desk buzzed.

'There's a Detective-Inspector Walters from Scotland Yard just arrived to see you, sir.' His secretary was as unruffled as ever. Gardener had never ceased to admire her equilibrium; he thought she would have made a first class newscaster. Sometimes he thought that he relied on her too much, put her in the firing line and hid behind her.

'Give me five minutes, Joan,' he said. Because I need a breather. Because I'm playing the waiting game the way bishops and chief constables play it. Because Walters was going to be the joker in the pack from here on, assigned to special duties so that you couldn't give him orders, he would do his own thing and damn you if you didn't like it.

And most disconcerting of all, the Scotland Yard detective would be armed, trained to hunt down terrorists and assassins with all the cunning and ferocity of a beast of prey. Which frightened Chief Superintendent Clive Gardener far more than did bishops and chief constables. Or the Antichrist.

CHAPTER THREE

'He's gone.' There was relief in Benjamin's voice as he slipped an arm around Penny's shoulders. 'He just hitched a ride to the Chase and now he's taken off to wherever he's going. Good riddance, the bum gave me the creeps. The last thing we wanted was him around tonight . . . '

Penny stiffened. The last thing she wanted to be reminded of was tonight, the Summer Solstice. She didn't want any part of it, she remembered last year only too well. She peered into the gathering dusk, tried to will herself to make out a lithe silhouette wearing a broad brimmed hat, strolling nonchalantly back to the campsite. But there was no sign of Haggard. His rucksack was gone from the bus, too, and that was an indication that Benjamin spoke the truth. The man who called himself Haggard was gone, and the chances were that they would never set eyes on him again. She experienced a sadness, almost an urge to cry.

'I don't expect we'll ever see him again,' Benjamin seemed to read her thoughts. 'I'd just like to know what he was up to, though.'

She did not reply. In an odd sort of way she had been attracted to Haggard. She only realized it now that he was gone. Sure, he was good looking but it went deeper than that; it was his self-assurance, his confidence. He was the kind of man a girl could feel safe with. And scared at the same time. Which was crazy. Maybe it was best that he had just walked away like he had, had not even said good-bye.

Over on the other side of the clearing some of the hippies were collecting dead branches, stacking them in the manner children built a Guy Fawkes bonfire. Penny shuddered. They were preparing the ritual fire, it would be no different from last time; she should have left the convoy days ago, abandoned them all, Benjamin, too. Now it was too late. Oh, if only Haggard had stayed, it would not have been so bad then. Which, again, was crazy, because there was no way the ritual would be any different, with or without the man in the black fedora. Except that she felt safer when he was around.

The landscape was wooded, conifer belts planted in symmetrical blocks as though the foresters were hell bent on destroying natural beauty. A valley with a wide stream running through it, deep in places, cold clear water that tasted good when you were thirsty. Silver birch lined the banks, self-sets that sprung up and matured, attempting to defy the artificiality of commercial forestry. Earlier in the day Penny had glimpsed a herd of deer, magnificent wary beasts which had leaped up and darted into the undergrowth the moment they caught her scent, gone within seconds as if they had never been.

'They shoot deer here, don't they?' She spoke her thoughts aloud, felt her companion's fingers dig deep into her flesh in sudden anger.

'They call it culling,' Benjamin grunted. 'They give you every reason under the sun why they have to do it. But they always avoid the truth, that venison fetches a high price. Jeez, three hundred deer in something like twenty-five thousand acres, and they need culling! They don't take into account what the poachers kill; that in itself would be a sufficient cull *if* it was necessary.'

'And they don't even use the skins for vellum these days, they waste them,' Penny wished that she had not spoken. Benjamin was edgy, in one of his moods.

'I should bloody think they don't!' His grip almost made her cry out. 'It's bad enough cutting down trees just to make paper. One way or another we're destroying this planet, the forests will soon be all gone and with it the oxygen we breathe, there won't be any habitat left for birds and animals. The fools ignore the danger signs. It'll soon be too late, if it isn't already. But they'll pay for it, I'll do my small bit towards that!'

'D'you think destroying the Lichfield Gospels will make any difference?' She twisted her body, tried to drag herself free of him but he was too strong for her.

'Sshh!' His face was thrust close to her own, his lips drawn back into a bestial snarl. 'Stupid girl! Why don't you go into the city and announce to the crowds what we're here for?'

'You're hurting me!' She cringed from the maddened fury in his expression.

'Trees and bushes have ears.' He glanced furtively about him, but if anybody had been hiding within earshot, it was too dark by now to spot them. 'Of course it will make a difference,' whispering now, his breath fetid with the stench of drugs. 'It's not like breaking into an abattoir or a fur store, that only makes local news. The Gospels are world famous, worth millions. It'll make national headlines and people will see that we mean business.'

'We?' Penny overcame her fear. 'You and who else? There's nobody but you and me know why we've come to Lichfield. I don't like it, Benjie. They'll be guarding the cathedral, it'll be a fortress.'

'They won't actually believe that anybody will be foolish enough to have a go at the Gospels.' He spoke even lower, looked round again. 'If we planned to steal them, yes, I'd agree with you that it was crazy, but we'll be in a crowd, I only need to get within a few yards of them . . . ' His eyes seemed to glow redly in the deepening darkness. 'This is the crossroads, Pen. I asked you once before and I'm asking you again now. Have you got cold feet? Do you want to opt out now, before it's too late?'

'No.' Her answer lacked conviction but she feared her lover's wrath had she replied in the affirmative. She was unsure. It had sounded fine talking about it, but out here in the wilderness, only miles from their goal, the whole thing had become terrifying. 'I'm only being . . . practical, Benjie.'

'Well, leave the practicalities to me.' He loosed his hold on her. 'You're sure you haven't mentioned it to any of the others?'

'Of course I haven't. But maybe they've already guessed.'

'Why should they?' Accusing, doubting her, his thick fingers threatening to grab her again.

'No reason except that others have talked about it in the camps before. There's a lot would like to destroy the Gospels but nobody thinks it's possible.'

'Well, I'm about to show them that it is. Which is one of the reasons why I had my suspicions about that Haggard fellow.'

'You've changed your opinion, you think that he might be a pig after all?'

'No-oo.' Benjamin began rolling a smoke. 'He stands out too much to be fuzz. If he was one, you wouldn't spot him in a crowd, he'd blend into it, be like one of us. I'm thinking that maybe he has plans of his own that might just be the same as ours.'

'Oh!'

'Which is why I'm now thinking that maybe it isn't such a good idea that he's done a runner. At least whilst he was around we could keep an eye on him. He could be just anywhere right now. Which means we can't hang around too long, we may have to bring our own plans forward. If Haggard makes an attempt on the Gospels and fails, as he will fail, then he'll screw it up for us. There won't be a second chance, the fuzz will see to that.'

'He was probably just a drifter.' She tried to speak casually, accepted the offered drag on Benjamin's cigarette and handed it back to him; she felt more relaxed already. If she ran out on her lover then that was the end of her supply of grass. 'But he's gone and that's that. I'm going to have a stroll down to the stream, see if I can spot those deer again.'

'Then don't be long.' He hesitated, suspicion in his narrowed eyes. 'Because we need you tonight, Pen. You haven't forgotten what night it is, have you?'

'I haven't forgotten.' She was glad that it was now almost fully dark or else he might have noticed that she was trembling. Midsummer rites could be a terrifying experience for a girl when her companions in the ritual were high on drugs. 'I'll be back, I promise.'

She did not hurry, stood watching Benjamin until the darkness swallowed him up. She admired him for his ideals, but now he was becoming obsessional, fanatical. It was like living with a time-bomb, you never knew when it might blow up. He was just crazy enough to launch a kamikaze attack on those ancient parchments, not caring if the police arrested him so long as he defaced or destroyed his target.

Just the soft rippling of the stream, the soughing of the warm night breeze through the silver birches and rhododendrons. Penny stopped to listen, she could not even hear the sounds of the hippy camp now. She almost convinced herself that she was the only person left alive in a civilization which had been hell-bent on self-destruction. Just herself and the deer which would not be culled ever again. Cities would decay and crumble, Nature would reclaim that which was rightfully hers. The cycle would begin again. It was a lovely thought.

There was no sign of the deer. She stared at the shadows, imagined all kinds of shapes, willed them to be fallow deer coming to the stream to drink, holding her breath in case they heard her and fled. Something moved in a clump of bracken behind her. She tensed. If it wasn't a deer then perhaps it was a fox or a badger, or even just a rabbit emerging from its warren to graze now that night had fallen.

'Hallo.'

Penny did not start, just froze, a kind of petrification that numbed every muscle in her body – if she had attempted to cry out no sound would have escaped her lips. Because, in the same moment that she heard that voice in the darkness, she recognized it. Her breathing was shallow, her skin prickled, her heart began to pound like a pneumatic drill deep in her chest. She heard the undergrowth rustling with light footsteps and, even before she saw the silhouette against the saffron sky with its early stars, she had anticipated that fedora pulled down to hide the pale features in dark shadows, the lithe body with the rucksack swinging on its shoulder strap.

'It's only me,' Haggard spoke softly, apologetically, 'I'm sorry if I startled you. I was hoping to catch a glimpse of the deer, but I rather think that the noise from the camp back there has driven them to another watering hole.'

'Yes,' she scarcely recognized her own voice, 'I was looking for them, too.'

He was close now and she smelled him as the deer might have scented herself, not the unwashed body odours of her companions on the bus but instead the smell of a male body that was clean; it was more heady than the drag she had had from Benjamin's cigarette.

'I . . . I thought you had left.' She spoke because she felt the need to say something, was aware of the sheer relief in her voice.

'I had. Temporarily. Now I'm back. Don't you think it's rather risky wandering about a place like this on your own after dark?'

'It's safe enough here, not like the city. But I was thinking of returning to the camp anyway.' Penny regretted her words for, in spite of her reservations, her nagging fear of this stranger, there was something about him which made her want to remain out here with him. His face, still hidden in the shadow of his hat, was within inches of hers. She tried to will his lips to move in on her own, upturned them in readiness.

He said, 'I'll walk back with you.'

'Are you sure you want to go back?' she asked as he fell into step with her.

'Why do you say that?'

'Because . . . ' Maybe if Haggard had been going someplace else, she would have gone with him. 'Because . . . tonight it's the Summer Solstice. There will be big celebrations, rites which you might not understand. I don't, but I still have to take part in them. You'd be better keeping your distance.'

'Maybe I'll just watch from a distance,' he replied, and then neither of them spoke again. There was so much to say, too much to be said in the short time it would take them to reach the camp. Much to her relief, as they emerged into the clearing, Penny saw that Benjamin was sleeping soundly in the front seat of the bus. Some of the others were still sitting around the embers of the communal cooking fire, smoking and talking; the huge beacon was still unlit. The night was young yet.

Haggard deposited his bag on the seat which he had claimed for his own and Penny watched him go back outside. Maybe he was going to make himself scarce, watch unseen from a distance. The thought sent tiny shivers creeping up her spine.

The big bonfire crackled as the flames licked at the dry brushwood, sent showers of sparks high into the night sky. It might have been the start of a public fireworks display in some recreational park except that the flickering firelight glinted on naked, dancing bodies. A circle of men and women, holding hands, mutterings that were becoming a chant as the heat drove them back another few yards.

'Let the flames dispel noxious dragons that copulate in the air and drop their poisonous seed into drinking wells!' Benjamin shouted, pointed defiantly skywards and a forest of upraised arms followed suit.

All eyes were on him, the watchers in awe of this red-bearded giant draped with a chaplet of mugwort and vervain, his eyes hidden amidst the bunch of larkspur which adorned his head.

Penny stepped forward, threw some herbs on to the fire, saw how they were devoured instantly. Arms aloft, she cried in a shrill voice: 'May all our ill luck depart and be burned with these.'

She backed away, felt the lusting eyes of the menfolk burning into her with a heat that scorched her, had her trembling visibly. Tonight was the only night of the year that Benjamin would let any of the others touch her. He had offered her as a sacrifice, just as she had sacrificed those sweet-smelling herbs.

She knew that Haggard was watching. She stared into the darkness beyond the fireglow in the vain hope of seeing him. Oh, Haggard, why don't you come and take me, too?

Her senses swam, she didn't care any longer, did not resist the eager hands that reached for her and swept her up. Now they would dance. And dance. A frenzy that would last until their strength gave out and they sank down on to the grassy floor. Then the men would crawl, drag their exhausted bodies over the ground, calling on every last reserve so that they might enjoy her shapely body. And afterwards they would sleep where they rolled until the chill of a new day, a new era, revived them . . .

Morning. Penny groaned, the grey dawn light hurt her eyes, it was painful just to look around. Some of her companions, her lovers of the night, still slept. But most of them were already at the cold remnants of the solstice fire, bathing themselves in its dead ashes, cleansing their bodies after a night of fornication.

God, she felt sick, she heaved, almost vomited. Her feeling was supposed to be one of elation, instead it was of degradation. Whore of the dragons, you have taken their poisonous seed.

She began to crawl on all fours, headed towards that mountain of ash whence grey clouds rose and drifted in the early morning breeze as if to hide the scene from mortal eyes. She grabbed a handful, began rubbing it into her skin; it felt gritty, dirty. Later she would go and bathe in the stream but for these worshippers the ceremony had not yet ended; she must see it through.

She thought again about Haggard, cringed because

he must surely have witnessed her night of promiscuity. Perhaps he had already left in disgust, for good this time. The thought was disconcerting, frightening. I have to know. Now.

Somehow she managed to stand, walked falteringly in the direction of the bus. None heeded her, it would be several hours before their drugged minds were functioning again.

Benjamin was back in the front seat, sleeping soundly, a grey sprawled heap of obesity, his bulging abdominal fat quivering as he snored. Penny spared him one glance of undisguised contempt and then her thoughts returned to the man in the black fedora.

Haggard was not here, he had left in disgust just as she had feared. Despair, and then hope as she noticed the rucksack on his seat. He would not have left without his belongings. He had gone again but, as before, he would be back.

That was when she began to tremble because she knew what she was about to do, knew that there was no way that she could stop herself. Curiosity, perhaps, she did not try to explain it, as her shaking, ash-grimed fingers reached for that bag.

She had no right to do it, she hated herself for it, almost changed her mind, but by the time she had pulled the zip fastener on Haggard's rucksack it was too late. Even then she might have zipped it back up and lied to herself that it had never been more than a guilty thought at the back of her mind. Had there been some clothes stuffed on the top, anything, she would have done no more than glance furtively inside, a kind of guilty compulsion to satisfy her inquisitiveness. She told herself all this, almost believed it.

But there was nothing obstructing her view of the .38 Smith & Wesson which lay on top of a folded shirt inside the bag.

CHAPTER FOUR

Don Devereux obtained a sense of satisfaction from the fact that his popularity with the Sealed Knot and the various local amateur dramatic players had plummetted. Had this not been the case, and it invariably had in the majority of pageants which he had organized in the past, then he would have been slightly concerned because popularity was never the handmaiden of efficiency.

His height was somewhat belied by his thick neck and bulky frame, bone structure and muscle which had no room for surplus flesh. Slightly stooped shoulders gave him the appearance of some deformity, yet this had been his forte for many of the roles which he had played in national celebrations throughout the continent. Heavy-featured, his thick eyebrows lent his expression a permanent scowl, the face of a man who would accept nothing less than perfection, and even then he would not acknowledge it. Few confronted him openly, mostly they complained out of earshot, huddled together to whinge in whispered tones, started guiltily when he moved towards them.

Devereux's passport stated that his nationality was French, yet his voice was cultured with no give-away accent; he spoke both English and German fluently, faltered only slightly with Italian and Spanish. An entrepreneur of pageantry, he had risen to immediate fame with his success in the French bicentennial celebrations, and received a number of commissions immediately following his re-staging of the storming of the Bastille. He had had to consult a map in order to ascertain the geographical location of Lichfield, had almost rejected the offer to elevate the Festival to an event of national importance; his financial demands had bordered on the outrageous, even by his own new standards, but they had been accepted.

And at this stage of the proceedings his employers were well pleased; they had congratulated him on the clockwork-like precision of the various processions, the jousting tournament and the archery contest. He had truly resurrected the city's heritage, the mayor had stated at a civic luncheon. Now the grand finale was only five days away and, in Devereux's opinion, there was much work still to be accomplished.

The first full dress rehearsal of the siege of the cathedral had been a shambles. This was partly due to the time limit imposed upon the enactment; they had to be finished by 4.30 so that evensong could take place as scheduled. The dean had flatly refused to postpone the service for another hour, had complained of loss of revenue by the crowds being barred from the Close. Two and a half hours, Don Devereux pouted his thick lips, was no time at all in which to mould this rabble of would-be actors into any semblance of professionalism.

There had been a delay right at the start. An unmarked police car had arrived on the scene and a detective-constable from the West Midlands Firearms Department had shown his credentials and demanded to check the muskets.

'The Firearms Amendment Act, 1988.' The officer was officious, took an obvious delight in using his authority and delaying the start of the rehearsal. 'We have to check all weaponry.'

'*Mon Dieu*!' Devereux took a deep breath, let it out slowly. 'They are antiques, they make a bang and a smoke, nothing more. Blank charges. A ball would be to the danger of the shooter, would probably burst the barrel.'

'Nevertheless, we have to check them.' The policeman moved over to where the six flintlocks were propped against the old well. 'Also, I require to see your black gunpowder licence.'

The detective's ballistical expertise was, quite clearly, limited to modern weapons. A musket was inverted, shaken, but nothing spilled out of the barrel. He used a pencil torch, squinted inside in an attempt to find a lodged leaden ball of lethal potential, but in the end reluctantly agreed that the rifle was unloaded. The creased certificate was scrutinized carefully, purchases of crude gunpowder checked against the contents of the cannister. All was in order, he admitted grudgingly, and departed.

Devereux looked towards the lorry which was parked in front of the old school house where a tarpaulin covered two cannons that were due to be unloaded tomorrow. Incidentals, props, like the muskets you took them for granted, concentrated on the important matters; time was at a premium, he was behind with his schedule.

The local actors resented the fact that Devereux had taken the part of Lord Grenville Brooke for himself. Subconsciously they also hated him because he was going to conduct a Parliamentary attack on their revered cathedral; he was the enemy, whichever way you looked at it. They had a greater knowledge of local history than this outsider, this *foreigner*, seized upon trivial inaccuracies with relish whereas the overall splendour of the occasion was the criteria. The crowds would flock here to see a battle of magnitude enacted with passion and realism, not some petty skirmish.

Nigel Jameson of the Sealed Knot was a true professional, Devereux conceded that grudgingly. The man clearly thought that he could have organized the spectacular better than this hired Frenchman, but not one word of dissent escaped those thin lips which rarely smiled. The man just got on with his job, performed it with all the talent he possessed. Yet, Don Devereux knew what the other was thinking, hated him for it.

The amateurs did not count for much in Devereux's estimation, they were here to make up the numbers and do as they were told; he refused to be riled by their clumsiness. Carruthers, a lawyer by profession, had an air of conceit about him, wanted to be in the spotlight although he had only a minor supporting role. Philip Page, the estate agent, was used to selling everything except himself. The most minor task was turned into one of significance, an arrogance in everything he did which seemed to impress his fellow amateurs. But not Don Devereux; on the Big Night he was determined that Page would be insignificant. But the man who rankled him most was Ron Borg, a bespectacled prematurely greying man who worked in the gun trade. A craftsman in his own right, but not in acting.

God forbid, anybody would think that those damned muskets were the focal point of the whole performance! They were weapons, nothing more, used solely in Cromwellian times for shooting at the enemy, as were their modern counterparts today. They were not idols to be worshipped.

But Borg's interest transcended his profession, had

become an obsession with him. From the moment when the firearms had been delivered, loaned for the occasion by a private collector, Borg had been examining them at every opportunity, handling them lovingly.

'Beauties!' The gunsmith caressed one, mounted it to his shoulder and squinted along the shiny barrel, cocked the hammer with a resounding click. 'As true a weapon as you will find anywhere in the world today, it's only drawback the slowness to load and the single shot.'

'A museum piece.' There had been a faint sneer in Devereux's reply. 'Try firing it with a ball and it would blow up in your face. We shall only be firing powder and wads. Now, please, Mister Borg, put it down. I am assured that it is worth a fortune and I would hate to see it dropped and damaged.'

'I spend my life handling valuable guns!' There was anger in the sharp retort, in the eyes behind those heavy lenses and the hand gripping the ornate barrel tightened its grip until the knuckles whitened. 'I repair them, I have even made them. I engrave them and . . . I also shoot with them!'

'A true marksman!' Devereux gave a short laugh. 'It is perhaps fortunate then, Mister Borg, that we shall not be firing bullets in our siege! Please put the gun down, you will have ample opportunity to handle it at our next rehearsal, I assure you. Put it back. Now!' Devereaux raised his voice, turned towards the other players who were watching with more than a casual interest, possibly hoping for a confrontation between these two. 'We meet tomorrow morning at ten-thirty. Sharp. Please report in full costume. We have no time to waste.'

He watched them leave, noted their eagerness to be away from this place. Devereux had hoped for their full co-operation, all he could expect was their time. Jealousy, basically. You positioned a man, explained to him exactly what was expected of him, and he did what he was asked. Reluctantly, almost. God, were these people not interested in history? Were they totally devoid of the vital ingredient, *passion*?

'May I remove the muskets for safe keeping, sir?'

God in heaven, was everybody obsessed with those damned muskets! Devereux turned slowly, saw Edwards, one of the cathedral guides assigned to help the actors. An insignificant fellow, like the players he simply obeyed orders and resented those who issued them, just did as he was told.

'Yes, thank you, Edwards.' Devereux forced a smile. 'We've finished with them for today. Is that a royal box those men are building over there?'

Edwards followed the other's pointing finger to where a wooden construction of raised benches, with a platform above it, stood beneath the mighty trees outside the deanery driveway. It might have been a bandstand. Or a performer's stage at an outdoor pop concert. 'It's for the guests of honour at the siege, sir. You know, this Polish chap and his mates who are coming to watch the finale, the fellow all the fuss is about in the papers.'

'Oh, yes, of course,' Devereux nodded. 'I read something about it, the Polish premier visiting Britain, coming here because he feels he has a duty to visit the graves of his fellow countrymen killed in the war.'

'Their *memorial*, sir. Not their graves. The only graves he's visiting are those of the Krauts killed on British soil and their remains interred on Cannock Chase, which is quite close to here. Lord knows why we've got to 'ave them, they was our enemy, it was kill or be killed, and they killed enough of our blokes!'

'The war finished almost half a century ago.' Devereux watched the other through narrowed eyes, this seemingly humble and obedient servant of the cathedral was pale, trembling, struggling to hold the anger in check which simmered inside him. 'We can't go on bearing grudges, you know.'

'The Nazis killed my father, sir,' a Cockney accent was discernible now. ''E was shot trying to escape from one of their prison camps. And the papers reckon this Polish guy's uncle was a Nazi and that 'e's buried up there on the Chase, too. They say also somethin' about 'im bein' descended from a Pole they locked up in a loony bin in this country a hundred years ago, suspected of being Jack the Ripper. And we 'ave to 'ave 'is kind sittin' up there in pomp and ceremony whilst we performs for 'im! Makes yer sick!'

'I think you're being a little fanciful.' Devereux turned away. 'If it's any consolation to you, Edwards, my father was killed in the German occupation of Paris. But I'm a professional and I'm still prepared to perform for the Polish premier. We can't go on blaming generation after generation for the sins of their forefathers, can we?'

The musket barrels clinked as Edwards carried them away. Damn it, people were getting worked up over nothing, threatening to spoil a spectacular with their grudges. Don Devereux glanced at his watch. It was a quarter to five and the bell was tolling to summon the eventide worshippers. The barriers were open, crowds were moving into the Close, sightseers who thronged to marvel at the architecture of this cathedral yet overlooked the purpose of its existence. It was first and foremost a tourist attraction, God's temple came a poor second.

Devereux had not intended to go inside the

cathedral, certainly not still wearing his costume, the plush cassock and the steel helmet with its five gilt bars. Bystanders were eyeing him with curiosity, a verger stared at him, made as if to say something but changed his mind. Grenville Brooke was the sworn enemy of Lichfield, his memory was a blot upon this holy city. Even a lookalike was not welcome here. But there were no rules regarding dress for visitors.

The Frenchman told himself that he had gone into the cathedral for the purpose of research. To walk his stage, to absorb the atmosphere. If anybody stopped him that was what he would tell them; he did not have to, he did not need to, but he would vindicate his presence here if necessary.

People were walking on tip-toe, conversing in whispers which echoed into husky shouts. The organ was playing, a congregation of some fifty or sixty were seated in the nave awaiting the commencement of evensong.

Devereux followed a trickle of tourists, heard a monotone voice in the distance, a recited lecture coming from the small Chapter House; it might even have been a tape grinding out its last recording of the day.

'. . . here we witness the superb skill of the scribe, colour is of no great importance on this particular page. The outline of the cross, which is today known as St Chad's Cross . . .'

Devereux mingled with the small audience, saw a grey-haired man in a dark suit pointing to a number of framed vellum pages set on a series of stands. Superbly decorated pages, perhaps of oriental origin, lettering that was outstanding in its beauty yet needed the help of an interpreter to convey its meaning to the layman tourist.

'. . . the cathedral was badly damaged by

Cromwell's troops during the Civil War . . . ' The speaker noticed the newcomer, frowned as he saw and recognized the costume of one of the offenders to whom he referred, ' . . . but the Gospels were removed before the commencement of the siege, and hidden, we know not where. Suffice that they were saved and returned some thirty years later, but we do not know for sure whether there were two or just one volume. Now, here we see the end of St Matthew's Gospel . . . '

But Don Devereux, international organizer of festivals and pageants, principal actor by his own casting, was no longer listening. For just as his own theatrical costume had aroused the interest of bystanders, so now was his own attention diverted by one whose dress did not conform to that of the conventional tourist.

It was the intensity of the other's expression which he noticed first, the way those pallid features were rigid with concentration, oblivious of all else. He saw how those pale blue eyes stared fixedly at the vellum pages as though obsessed with them.

Only then was the Frenchman aware of the wide-brimmed black hat, outrageous headgear worn in defiance of custom within the hallowed walls of God's temple, and the tight-fitting dark denim clothing which in the gloom of this holy place had a sinister impact.

Devereux stepped back a pace, experienced a sudden pang of fear, shrugged it off in an instant. It was just the shock of coming upon one so deathly pale, dressed almost in funereal attire, he tried to tell himself. Shock effect for the sake of it.

The man in black had not even noticed him, he had been too absorbed in the St Chad's Gospels, an obsession that was on a parallel with Ron Borg's fixation with weaponry. Devereux dragged his gaze away, was suddenly aware that he was sweating, and not just because of his heavy cassock and helmet; he was trembling as though with the beginnings of a fever.

He turned away, hurried from the Chapter House with steps that were heavy and echoed an undue haste in spite of the anthem which filled the nave. He had to restrain himself from running headlong for the sunlight which slanted in through the open west door.

Outside in the oppressive heat of the afternoon sunshine he felt faint. Only then did he finally admit to himself that he was the victim of an inexplicable, illogical terror. A fear of that stranger who wore a black fedora and for some reason was totally obsessed with the Lichfield Gospels. He sank down on to a bench, trembled violently. It had not *just* been the unknown tourist, he was only part of it; it was an indescribable atmosphere of sheer evil which had lingered in that place, lurked in the gloomy recesses of the Chapter House, as though some terrible evil force had infiltrated the House of God. It was as though Satan himself had returned to take his revenge upon He who had cast him down into hell.

Which was nonsense, Don Devereux told himself, but he continued to tremble for some time afterwards.

CHAPTER FIVE

'Man, I think you've got something to tell me.'

Haggard seemed at first not to have heard, methodically turning the slices of potato in the pan which he held over the fire. His customary fedora shaded his face so that the watching Penny was unable to see his expression. Her breathing had gone suddenly shallow, her temples were pounding as she glanced from Haggard to Benjamin and back again. Oh, God, this was the confrontation which she had been dreading. She would never forget the shock of finding that gun in Haggard's bag, the knowledge that her intuition had been right about him, that he was far more dangerous than she had sensed. She had left that pistol untouched, zipped it up in the rucksack again, had even considered telling Benjamin about her discovery. No, that would have been disloyal to this stranger who thrilled and excited her. But if anything happened then she would have to live with her conscience for the rest of her life. Maybe he was a bank robber, a murderer on the run.

'I beg your pardon?' Haggard looked up, lifted his breakfast clear of the flames, laid the pan on the ground to cool. 'What am I supposed to tell you?'

'I think you know as well as I do.' Benjamin towered over the other, an angry red-bearded giant, the veins in his neck protruding and throbbing. 'The time for pussy-footing about is over. You've accepted our hospitality for almost two weeks and now I reckon it's time we put our cards on the table. What's your game, feller?'

Haggard looked up, shifted his weight to his other knee, tipped his hat back so that his features were clearly visible in the morning sunlight. Neither shock nor anger, just puzzlement. Had it not been for that gun, Penny might still have thought him to be a harmless, eccentric drifter. But there was no getting away from the fact that he carried a pistol; she had touched it, shuddered and flinched as her fingertips had stroked the cold black steel.

'I'd be grateful if you would put me in the picture.' Haggard was unruffled, a faint smile creased the corners of his mouth. 'If I've inadvertently done something wrong, then please tell me and I'll do my best to put it right.'

Fifty yards away the inhabitants of the hippy nomad settlement were clustered in a noisy group. Shouting, laughing, a strange mixture of gaiety and anger as they busied themselves making banners, tearing old sheets into strips, some of them holding the ragged material taut whilst others sprayed slogans with aerosol paint cannisters.

REMEMBER GDANSK: JARUZELSKI, MASS MURDERER. KOSMINSKI THE RIPPER.

'Never mind them.' Benjamin saw Haggard's gaze flick over the gathering. 'There's things you and me've got to sort out. Right now!'

'All right.' Haggard was still relaxed, meeting the other's hostile gaze unflinchingly. 'I think you'd best go ahead and tell me what's the trouble instead of talking in riddles.'

Benjamin took a long breath, his broad torso seemed to inflate to gigantic proportions. His nostrils flared and his huge fists bunched menacingly.

'You're planning to steal the Gospels, aren't you, Haggard, or whatever your bloody name is?'

'Gospels?' For a fleeting moment the smaller man's expression was one of incredulity. 'Oh, you mean the ones in the cathedral?'

'I do, and you bleedin' well know it. Like I said, stop this arsing around. I know you've been there, sussing the place out. You were *seen* there, Haggard, by *me*, so don't get lying about it.'

Haggard laughed suddenly, a peal of genuine mirth that had Penny's skin goosepimpling; anywhere else his response would have defused a potentially explosive situation. Maybe right now it might have done just that had it not been for the .38 she had found in his bag. She would never be able to trust him again, but he still held a sinister fascination for her. And now that was doubly frightening.

'Well?' Benjamin advanced a step, scuffed some loose ash with his boot and sent a cloud of dust up into the air.

'I might ask *you* what you were doing in the cathedral.' Haggard's voice was low, barely audible. 'Frankly, the idea of stealing the Gospels never entered my head. I find them rather interesting. I also find this conversation quite hilarious.'

'You'll be laughing on the other side of your bloody face in a second!'

'Look, this gets crazier by the minute.' Haggard rocked back on his heels. 'I go into the city, I visit the cathedral, I listen to a lecture on the Gospels, and now you're accusing me of planning to steal them. Jeez, it's laughable, there are police and security men all over the place, you wouldn't stand a chance. But I'm intrigued to know where you got this notion from.'

Penny had never seen Benjamin uncertain of himself before. In the wrong, certainly; many times, but he never faltered, right or wrong. He always blustered, bluffed, bulldozed his way through anybody or anything which stood in his way. Except now. His hands unclenched, his thick fingers straightened out; his face was still suffused with blood but now it was because embarrassment was taking over from anger. He stepped back the pace that he had advanced, averted his eyes from Haggard's unwavering stare. He looked to Penny as if pleading with her to come to his rescue.

'I . . . we thought that . . .'

'Anybody can make a mistake.' Haggard began forking slices of fried potato out of the pan on to an enamel plate. 'It just beats me why you thought I was going to nick the Gospels. I mean, suppose that was my plan, would it really make one helluva big difference to you? I might have it in mind to steal the crown jewels, would that inconvenience you any? Like you said at the start, it's best if we get things straight, and now that we've done just that I'd like to eat my breakfast uninterrupted. That okay with you?'

'If you want those Gospels, then go get 'em,' Benjamin's voice was husky, quavering. 'But what bothers me is what you might do with 'em after you'd stolen 'em.'

'I'm sorry?'

'You're awful thick, man. Look at it this way, anybody clever enough to steal the Gospels has got a problem and a half on his plate. There's rich bent collectors who'd give you a million cash for them, but the Gospels can't ever come to light, they've got to be locked away in secret forever. And that won't help *our* cause.'

'Perhaps I am thick,' Haggard smiled wanly, chewed on a potato slice, 'because for the life of me I can't see what you're driving at.'

'All right.' Benjamin thrust his head forward, his voice now a gruff whisper. 'Maybe you are lying to me, chap, and you do have it in mind to steal those Gospels. Fine . . . *so long as you destroy 'em when you've got 'em, because I intend somehow to damage 'em so much they'll never be any good to anybody afterwards!*'

'Oh!' Haggard's face registered mild surprise, the kind of disbelief a loyal son might show upon hearing some outrageous statement from a parent with senile dementia. 'But, forgive me, what do you stand to gain by destroying or defacing them?'

'Jesus, you really are thick!' Benjamin's ruddy features took on an even deeper hue and contorted into a mask of rage. 'Each one of those pages was once an animal's skin. A poor, defenceless dumb creature, slaughtered so that some hypocritical so-called saint could scratch his balderdash all over them! That's the Church, Christianity, for you! Thou shalt not kill except when it suits you. Get me?'

The other nodded, his mouth full. Penny was not sure if Haggard was merely humouring her lover, it was impossible to tell. Finally, Haggard said, 'Fair enough, if that's how you feel, but those animals were killed well over a thousand years ago.'

'A thousand, ten thousand, what's the difference?' Benjamin's eyes seemed to protrude with his fanatacism, like bubbles that would stretch until they burst. 'They were slaughtered needlessly, just as animals are murdered today, so that carnivores who have the cheek to call themselves humans can eat their flesh. No difference, my friend, except that those creatures killed for the Gospels are suffering the degradation of being exhibited day in, day out, for tourists to gawp at. We once broke into a slaughter-house, Pen and I, sprayed all the carcasses with paint so that they were unfit for human consumption. It made the papers, just a half column on page nine. But *this* will make the headlines of every newspaper in Britain and Europe, possibly the States as well, and then folks will realize that the animal liberation movement is not to be trifled with! Man, do you bloody understand now?'

'I get your point,' Haggard nodded, forked another piece of potato into his mouth. 'Best of luck to you, but I can assure you, here and now, that I have not the slightest intention of attempting to steal the Lichfield Gospels.'

'Well, at least we've cleared that up, then.' Benjamin was visibly exhausted, this confrontation had drained him both mentally and physically. Maybe later in the day he would have one of his infrequent migraines. Then he grunted, 'Are you a vegetarian?' The question was intended to take Haggard by surprise, maybe a final attempt to wrong foot the man in black, to notch up a score against him.

'Spuds are vegetarian fare, aren't they?' Haggard answered and lapsed into silence.

Penny watched Benjamin slope away, disgruntled and beaten, his head hung low, his sandals scuffing dust all the way to the bus. 'He won't rest until the Gospels are destroyed,' she spoke softly, not looking at Haggard. Benjamin would sleep now, for five or six hours, and God help anybody who disturbed him.

'Everybody has their own ideals.' Haggard scraped his plate clean, looked up at her. 'He's entitled to his; me, I've got mine, the only difference being that I don't go thrusting them down other folks' throats. Seems like that crowd over there are getting a bit worked up over theirs, too.'

'You can't blame them, can you? I mean, it's a downright insult having a guy like this Kosminski visiting the country. There's people been massacred in Poland just for what they believe in, and here we are extending a VIP welcome to the bastard. They reckon his uncle was a Nazi and there are theories that he's descended from Jack the Ripper. So the papers say.'

'You don't want to believe half of what you read in the papers,' Haggard watched her through narrowed eyes, it was impossible even to guess what he was thinking. 'There'll be a few skirmishes, mini-riots, and some of your buddies will end up in a police cell. But it won't achieve anything because friend Kosminski will complete his tour and return to Poland to continue oppressing the masses. Nothing will have changed, whatever you say or do.'

'Unless . . . *somebody kills him!*'

Haggard tensed, his eyes jerked open, seemed to burn into her. 'What put that idea into your head? Is that Benjamin's next assignment? After he's vandalized the Gospels!'

She recoiled as if he had struck her a physical blow, such was the force of his words although he did not raise his voice above a hissed whisper.

'No! He wouldn't . . . *kill* anybody, Benjie's not like that. It was just something I read in the newspapers, along with all this Ripper stuff. They seem to think there might be an assassination attempt. They also say . . . ' she hesitated, 'that the Antichrist is coming to Lichfield!'

'The . . . *what*?'

'The Antichrist. Satan. The devil, whatever you like to call him.' She refrained from asking, 'Are you bloody thick?'

'They think up some rubbish to fill their rags with,' Haggard smiled again.

'The newspaper concerned had had an anonymous telephone call about it,' she added as if to vindicate herself. 'I'm only telling you what I read, that doesn't mean that I actually believe it.'

'I'd give the papers a rest if I were you.' He straightened up, adjusted his fedora, squinted in the bright morning sunlight. 'Too much reading is bad for you . . . even the Gospels.'

It was shortly after mid-day when Penny spied the convoy of police cars bumping their way up the rutted track from the road below the campsite; four of them, a red and white patrol car in the lead, followed by two panda cars and an unmarked van. Somebody shouted 'pigs!' but nobody moved; police raids were an occupational hazard of the hippy lifestyle.

The cars came on, not hurrying, swung round in an arc to park in an uneven line facing the shambles of dilapidated buses, vans and home-made tents. There was a pause before the officers got out, a kind of warning silence, almost a truce. Get the hell out of here, if you want to, it'll save us an awful lot of bother. But nobody moved.

Penny counted eight uniformed policemen, one of whom was a high-ranking officer, a chief inspector possibly, carrying a loud hailer in his hand, standing with it halfway to his mouth. Maybe he was mentally rehearsing his carefully prepared speech, she thought. The rear doors of the van opened and two more policemen emerged, Alsatian dogs leashed by their side. They walked across to the remains of the solstice fire, let the dogs sniff around it, eyed the ashes as though they expected to find the remains of a human sacrifice amongst it.

It's the fire that did it, Penny thought, it could be seen for miles around and they knew what it was. Black magic rites, human sacrifice, the minds had boggled. But the law had waited until the next day because they knew the end result would be the same. They would search the camp for drugs, it was easier to do it in the daylight. Then the media would jump on the bandwagon, write up lurid features on witchcraft and satanic rites, link it to the coming of the Antichrist. They had it made, given to them on a plate.

'We have today received an eviction order against you,' the leading officer announced through his megaphone. 'You are trespassing on private property . . . ' His words were drowned in a volley of catcalls from the banner-makers. 'I repeat, you are trespassing and you are given notice to move from this place within forty-eight hours. Failure to comply with this order will result in charges being brought against you. We are here to execute warrants to search your vehicles. Please stay where you are and do not attempt to obstruct police officers carrying out their duty.'

Penny felt herself starting to tremble. Her intuition had not failed her; the big fire had brought the fuzz on the run like night moths to a lighted lamp. Some of the hippies were voicing protests, resorting to obscenities as they proceeded to insult their visitors, but none of the sixty or so gathered in the centre of the camp made any move to resist. Perhaps if the big convoy, from whom they had parted company outside Stonehenge, had been here then there would have been trouble. As it was, nobody was going to risk having those dogs set on them.

She looked for Haggard, spotted him standing some twenty yards away, caught out in the open, a loner like he always was. There was no sign of Benjamin, he was probably still deep in an exhausted slumber inside the bus.

She found herself searching for his rucksack, straining her eyes in an attempt to spot it hanging from his shoulder. It was not there so it had to be in the bus, dumped on the seat where she had found it the other night. Oh, Christ, she started to panic inwardly, they're going to find that pistol and that will be big trouble for him and the rest of us. Drugs were an expected find in any police search of a peace convoy, but firearms were a thousand times more serious. Her legs felt almost too weak to support her body; she should have told Benjamin, he would have done something about it. Maybe stolen the gun, thrown it in the stream. He hated weapons in any form because he despised killing. But it was too late now.

The search took half an hour, no more. Nobody knew for certain what the police had found in the vehicles. Certainly they would seize drugs but they were unlikely to press charges, no more than they would prosecute for unlicensed, unroadworthy buses and vans. Because ultimately it would cost the taxpayer money and put an additional, unnecessary burden on the courts. As always, the policy was to harass and to evict, to pass the buck. Move 'em on, get 'em over the border into the next county.

The police emerged from the vehicles, their finds in green dustbin liners. They seemed to have let Benjamin sleep on undisturbed, Penny sighed her relief aloud. He was the one person who might have caused trouble, got himself arrested.

Haggard was still standing out there on his own, his back towards her so that she was unable to see his expression. The police *must* have found the gun, they couldn't miss it. They were grouping back by the cars, the inspector was turning towards the watchers, his megaphone going back up to his mouth. Penny tensed, but didn't want to hear. *We have found a firearm in a bag in the double-decker bus. Will the owner of this weapon please step forward. Failure to comply with this request will result in everybody being taken to the police station for questioning.*

I'm not going to grass on him, Penny stared defiantly at the senior officer. No way, even if it means us all going to prison. Her gaze switched to Haggard, it was all she could do to stop herself from running to him. She felt dizzy, thought that she was going to faint. Her vision blurred and a mist swirled in front of her eyes. Slowly, she lowered herself to the ground, sat down and put her head between her legs. Oh, God, they'll think the gun's mine, that I've fainted because . . .

Booming words but they were meaningless for her fogged brain. Any second she would throw up, pass out. She didn't give a damn if they came and took her away. So long as they didn't touch Haggard.

Possibly she had fainted briefly, she could not be sure. She heard the revving of engines, caught a faint whiff of exhaust smoke in the breeze and the pungent fumes seemed to revive her. Cautiously she raised her head, clawed at the coarse grass as another wave of dizziness engulfed her.

She wanted to shout her exuberance but only a croak escaped her lips, for the police were leaving, that convoy easing its way back down the rough track, the van in the rear. An incline swallowed them up one by one until they were hidden from her view.

Everybody was just standing about aimlessly, no show of anger, just the usual acceptance of a police raid. The law had taken any drugs they had found, anything which they considered might be used as an offensive weapon. Just anything, in fact. Even the banners were gone, the big one that had been strung out between two stakes to dry was no longer to be seen. The police were not going to risk a political embarrassment when the Polish premier arrived in the city. That was the reason behind this morning's search, to quell a riot before it began. And the scapegoats would be black magic rites and drugs. Now the tabloid newspapers would take over and have a field day.

Where was Haggard? She could not see him, experienced a sudden feeling of panic. Because of the gun and its consequences. Sheer relief when she saw him, over by the bus, nonchalantly washing his breakfast plate in a bucket of water.

Again she fought that overwhelming urge to run to him, a foolish, illogical reaction brought about by sheer relief. Nothing more, she tried to convince herself. For some reason they had not arrested him, maybe they would be back for him later, some kind of cat and mouse game. Or else they were satisfied with confiscating the pistol and were ducking out of a major confrontation with the hippies.

Penny made her way slowly, falteringly, towards the bus. Haggard did not look up as she passed him, the washing of his plate might for all the world have been the most important task he had ever undertaken.

She climbed the step, had to hold on to the rail until the sensation of vertigo had passed. Benjamin was lying full length across the front seat, his shirt pulled up out of his trousers so that the roll of grimed flesh spilling over his waistband was in full view. His mouth was open and he was snoring stentoriously. A sense of revulsion had her jerking her eyes away from him, seeing in her mind instead Haggard with his lithe figure and handsome pale face. A little shiver ran part of the way up her spine and then she was searching frantically, almost panic-stricken, for that canvas bag with its shoulder strap, which would not be here because the police had taken it away.

Her pounding heart missed a beat, started up again like an engine which had misfired because of a faulty plug lead. She clutched at a seat with a sweaty hand, held on. Her eyes were stinging from the perspiration that had run into them so she wiped them with her free hand, waited whilst her vision steadied.

An hallucination, doubtless caused by a combination of the heat and her ordeal. *The bag was there on the seat, exactly the way it had been the last time she had seen it.*

The material was smooth to her touch; she raked her fingernails along it but it was no fevered mirage, it stayed where it was. The zip was stiff, she had to get a grip on it, pull hard until it ran, suddenly speeded up.

She peered fearfully into the gap, tugged at it to widen it, hardly dared to look inside because by now she knew that the Smith & Wesson .38 would be there, lying snugly on top of a folded shirt, just the way it had been the last time.

Untouched.

CHAPTER SIX

Chief Superintendent Gardener tried not to show his aversion to being briefed by a detective-inspector, even if it was a Scotland Yard officer assigned to special duties. Age difference for a start. Walters would have been a rookie on the beat at the time when Gardener was promoted to chief inspector; the gap had narrowed but it had not yet closed. Basically, it was the difference between the metropolitan and a provincial force, a city policeman and a country copper. Both were doing the same job but this time it was the *big* one. Bigger even than the hunt for that child killer last year. Of international importance. Failure was not even contemplated, it was frightening to think about it.

Gardener complimented himself upon being a shrewd judge of character but now, sitting in his own office with Tim Walters on the other side of the desk, he was not so sure. He prided himself that he never forgot a face, but he had the feeling that if the Yard man walked out through the door he would be at pains to remember exactly what the other looked like. Because Walters was so nondescript, your typical man-in-the-street; mingle with the Festival crowds and you saw a hundred or more 'Walters', faces that bore no distinguishing features, mass-marketed casual clothing which your Mister Average wore seven days a week. Single him out, allow your gaze to wander and you lost him only to be replaced by a facsimile. Speak to him and his voice bore no accent, no mannerisms nor eccentricities; if he had any he kept them to himself.

The chief superintendent thought Walters was in his mid-to-late thirties; on the other hand, he could have been forty-five. Average build, an open-necked shirt and brown cords, scuffed sneakers on his feet. Mousey-coloured hair which, if combed in a different direction, would totally alter his appearance; give it a parting, exchange the casual clothes for a suit and tie, and you had your typical clerical worker, the nine-till-five cashier who struggled to meet his mortgage repayments and run a family car. If he found himself in financial difficulties he might fiddle the books. Comb the hair forward and you had . . . no, there was no category into which you could slot a special agent. His camouflage, his disguise, was the art of being able to blend into a background of humanity, lose himself amidst the masses.

'Kosminski arrived in London yesterday.' Walters crossed his legs, leaned back in his chair.

Gardener nodded, refrained from replying, 'I read it in the papers' or 'I saw it on the television news'. He had the feeling that his visitor was sussing him out, too. A sort of psychological duel, looking for reactions. Like a chief constable or a bishop did.

'Tomorrow he flies up to Birmingham International, there's a ceremony laid on at the NEC. I have to be there.' Detective-Inspector Walters did not elaborate, it was nothing to do with Lichfield what happened in Birmingham. 'The following day he comes here. By car. There will be a full police escort, your men take over at the county border, the A38 out of Sutton. That is when your problems begin.'

Gardener felt his stomach gripe, the feeling he got

sometimes when he drove to work after a full breakfast. 'There's a risk from the time Kosminski lands at Heathrow – before that even. There could be a bomb on the plane.' Which was bloody ridiculous, this was one plane which there would be no chance of any assassination group planting a bomb on.

'There's always a *risk*,' Walters smiled sardonically, 'but we've had a tip-off from a reliable source that the assassination attempt will be made in the Lichfield area. 'That is why I'm here.'

Gardener felt slightly sick, the other was intent on putting the ball right in the chief superintendent's court. Just in case they needed a scapegoat, if anything went wrong. It was no good quizzing Walters about the source of his tip-offs, Gardener would not even make a fool of himself trying. 'All right,' his voice sounded distant, 'I'll accept what you've told me.' He tapped a sheaf of papers on the desk in front of him. 'Here is a minute-by-minute schedule of Kosminski's itinerary from the time he arrives in this area until he departs on the morning after the final ceremony in the Close. The high risk areas are the Commonwealth Cemetery, the Katyn Memorial and possibly the mock siege of the cathedral. Those are the only occasions when he will be on public view. His hotel, any routes which he travels, and the three places mentioned will be heavily policed. The city centre has already been searched for hidden explosives, we have done everything according to the rule book. There will be a West Midlands Police Firearms Team present throughout.

'Only yesterday morning I ordered a search of the hippy encampment on Cannock Chase, a twofold motive. We have had a tip-off that there might be an attempt made on the Lichfield Gospels from an animal rights activist group, so it made sense to give the camp a good going over. We found nothing worth mentioning; my men confiscated some drugs and a number of provocative banners designed to embarrass us and sour relationships with the Polish delegation. There is a very strong feeling of resentment towards the Polish government amongst the hippies. We served an eviction order on the peace convoy, but I doubt very much whether we'll get rid of them before Kosminski and his entourage arrive. We don't have the manpower to shift them physically, we're over-stretched as it is.'

'I think we can forget that rabble,' Walters laughed contemptuously. 'They'll try to make trouble, throw things if they can get near enough to the cavalcade, but they don't stand a chance of doing anything serious. They're just a disgrace to this country and I'm surprised that you didn't move them on the moment they arrived.' A reprimand that might have come through the pecking order, Walters left to administer the rebuke, the hierarchy's disapproval.

'There wasn't time,' Gardener snapped irritably. 'By law we have to allow them forty-eight hours to move of their own free will. If they don't leave, then we can evict them. In theory. The problem is their deadline expires on the day Kosminski arrives in Lichfield. If we attempt an eviction then the security arrangements within the city will be weakened. So I'm afraid they'll have to stay put until after the Festival, by which time they will probably have moved on, anyway.'

Gardener pushed the sheaf of papers across the desk. Go on, take 'em, see for yourself that we haven't been sitting around on our backsides. 'And there's another problem cropped up, Inspector.' Trying not to gloat; we have our sources of information, too.

Walters waited, did not speak, not so much as a glimmer of curiosity in his expression.

Gardener averted his gaze. Christ, it sounded crazy, at least it had when the bishop had mentioned it the other afternoon.

'We've heard, via the bishop that the . . . the Antichrist is going to make his return to Earth during the Festival! The press have had a tip-off, too.'

'The . . . *what*?'

'You know, Satan . . . the devil . . . ' Oh, God Alive, it sounded like something out of a fantasy novel stretching the imagination to its limits. Clive Gardener swallowed, thought he might be blushing. He took a deep breath. 'I feel I have to inform you of everything that is going on, Inspector. Apart from Kosminski's safety, which is a priority, we have the possibility of an attempt being made on the Gospels, and . . . '

'And Old Nick turning up for the party.' Walters was shaking his head, ridiculing the other openly. 'Really, Chief Superintendent, we can't allow ourselves to be distracted by such farcical nonsense, we have to stick to reality. If Lucifer shows up then I'm afraid he'll have to leave the VIP spot to the Pole.'

'Quite.' Gardener laughed but it sounded forced. 'I merely mentioned it because the bishop is worried and now the press have latched on to it. Of course, I don't believe it's anything other than a hoax, but we must not overlook the fact that these hippies have been carrying out satanic rites at their camp. Like they tried to do at Stonehenge.'

'So?'

Oh, dear God: 'Well, these people are into all this black magic stuff and I'm thinking that there could well be a link between the Antichrist propaganda and the possibility of a plot to steal the Gospels. One up for the followers of darkness, if you get me. A red herring, if you like. Harmless, but a bloody nuisance and it's scaring the shit out of some folks.' The bishop, for a start.

'Whatever, that's your problem, Chief Superintendent. But surely, the easiest way to protect these Gospels is to lock 'em away!'

'I advised the bishop to do just that but, unfortunately, he flatly refuses. The Gospels are a tourist attraction, the loss in revenue to the cathedral and the city would be considerable if they were removed from public view. So, we have to provide a day and night police guard on them.'

'One man can take care of that.' Walters lit a cigarette. 'But Kosminski's safety is your priority as well as mine. Let me tell you something,' he leaned across the desk, 'I've had my briefing direct from the AC. If anything should happen, even an attempt on Kosminski's life, no matter how miserably it fails, it could have far-reaching percussions. Don't forget, this guy's a Russian puppet, as much as Jaruzelski, and if he got taken out on British soil, I dread to think of the consequences. So never mind your hippies and your Gospels, and your bloody Antichrist, we have every reason to believe that we are up against the most dangerous assassin in the business, and there's more than one country in the world that would benefit from an incident of this magnitude. If the worst comes to the worst, you can forget your pension, for starters!'

Clive Gardener dropped his hands below the desk, primarily so that Detective-Inspector Walters would not see how they trembled, also to clasp his churning stomach. He was not accustomed to being handed ultimatums; frequently he was asked to co-operate with other forces, had always given of his best, but there was the human error factor to take into consideration. Apparently, in this instance, it did not exist. There was no margin for mistakes, you were expected to forestall every conceivable possibility. Governments created problems, left others to solve them, clear up the mess. And there was always a scapegoat held in reserve. This time it was Chief Superintendent Gardener, Walters had left him in no doubt about that. The AC hand-picked his men, both winners and losers.

'I'll be around.' Walters scraped back his chair, and then he was gone through the door. The Chief Superintendent found himself trying to visualize what the other looked like. Just a vague memory of an inconsequential man, not even an individual, who reminded him in some abstract way of the jobbing plumber who had called last week to service the central heating system. And his train of thought embarked upon a much more frightening course; in all probability a top assassin perfected the same mode of anonymity.

As might the Antichrist if he existed. Which, at this very moment, the policeman was almost inclined to regard as a possibility. Gardener had an uneasy feeling that this holy city had suddenly become the focal point for evil forces that were beyond the ken of a once matter-of-fact chief superintendent of police. He experienced a sense of foreboding which was not wholly due to the impending visit of the Polish premier.

Premier Kosminski had maintained a dour expression throughout the short flight from Heathrow to Birmingham International airport. He neither spoke, nor had any wish to understand, the English language. That was the job of his interpreter. If a welcoming smile, a mere facial stretching was required to be reciprocated, then he left that to the latter also. The premier reluctantly engaged in handshakes, had taken the liberty of kissing the prime minister on the cheek as a subtle reminder that the Eastern Bloc countries were not prepared to pander totally to the customs of the western world. Dignity was maintained in formalities, he was an ambassador for communism, friendship was the brother of weakness.

At reception banquets he ate and drank with undisguised enthusiasm, ignored those who regarded polite conversation and speeches as the main purpose of such gatherings. The lapels of his charcoal grey suit were stained with spilled food which members of his entourage were responsible for removing after he had retired for the night. Only his deep-set eyes betrayed his true feelings to those who were brave enough to meet his gaze; contempt for the small banner-waving group of demonstrators who had screamed unintelligible obscenities during his tour of London before the police moved in on them, ridicule for the throng of sightseers lining the Strand, a workforce of idlers who would have been herded back to the shopfloors and docks in his own country.

The windows of his limousine were bullet-proof and constructed of one-way glass. A police escort rode in front and behind, he grunted his annoyance every time the cavalcade was halted by traffic signals. In Poland the streets would have been cleared of such obstructions, his passage unhindered. He fidgeted during each short wait, delays were not conducive to his self-importance, the status of a foreign dignitary was reduced to that of a local mayor.

Birmingham had been worse, a seething lack of organization. Momentary admiration for the

National Exhibition Centre turned to anger; a capitalist extravaganza at the expense of the people. Not that he had any sympathy for the masses – their role was to labour without dissent, to produce for the good of their country – but the money would have been better spent on factories for the manufacture of armaments. In the USSR, of course.

Yet, secretly, Kosminski envied what he saw, a thief eyeing the goods in a shop window with his thoughts turning to nightfall. When he pondered his eyes closed, so that those who did not know him well believed that he slumbered. Just as the Soviet Union slumbered throughout Gorbachev's reforms. Pseudo sleep.

He relied upon his own bodyguards, did not trust those assigned to him by the British. Michalek, his interpreter, was the only person whom he really trusted. Jaruzelski, he secretly feared, for the fate of a premier could be determined by a whim that did not necessarily have to come from the Kremlim. It was a fact of life. And death. You lived with it or died by it. But you learned to enjoy privileges whilst they were available.

Beneath his taciturn exterior, his apparent unwillingness to accept customs which incorporated freedom, he secretly relished his next destination. Silently, unobtrusively, he would pay homage to the graves of long-dead heroes, worship at the shrine of fourteen thousand of his own countrymen. His scheduled tour was, however, soured by the propaganda put about that his visit was intended to create a closer relationship between east and west. Jaruzelski had told him that personally, but surely the general neither believed that nor wished it to happen, he was merely conveying the empty words of a Kremlin façade. The Polish leader was not one to confide his innermost thoughts to anybody, not even his first minister.

Michalek had translated the final speech before they left the NEC. Just a small gathering, businessmen mostly; Kosminski fought against the temptation to yawn. Back in the Daimler he appeared to sleep, drowsy after a heavy lunch, soothed by the purr of the engine.

Some way outside Lichfield the cars slowed to a halt. Kosminski stirred, glanced out of the window through heavy lidded eyes, saw that the police escort was being changed. He did not understand why, was not interested enough to ask Michalek. In the distance, across the flat suburban plain, he saw three spires, a landmark even to a foreigner, recognized them from one of the guide books included in his itinerary package. Lichfield at last. An atheist, he accepted that holy places were necessary for the promotion of tourism; their importance was merely architectural, worship within them should be forbidden for it undermined the whole structure of communism.

It seemed an eternity before the convoy finally reached the city. The motorcycle cavalcade was clearing a way through the congested traffic, the pavements were crowded but the pedestrians seemed to be taking little interest in the limousine and its escort. Festival revellers, they had no time for visiting diplomats. A few shouted insults, a small band of protestors at Soviet oppression attempting to make their views heard, but the police moved them away. Kosminski wondered why the uniformed policemen did not use batons; a show of force was all that was necessary for keeping the rabble in order.

Suddenly he tensed, his eyes wide now and meeting those of one who stood on the edge of the pavement as though trying to penetrate the protective car window with a malevolent stare. Which was impossible, Kosminski was unable to suppress a tiny shiver, because one could not see through this glass from the outside. If their gaze had met, then it was in the premier's imagination.

The car was at a standstill, a white-coated police officer was lethargic in calling them forward. Kosminski was uneasy, glancing at Michalek and his bodyguards as if to reassure himself, mentally urging the chauffeur to drive on, to leave behind this disturbing spectre dressed in dark clothing and a broad-brimmed hat who stood amidst the crowds and glared with smouldering hatred. Kosminski refused to concede that there was anybody below the status of his own premiership who was capable of instilling even the faintest fluttering of disquiet in him.

Yet, this man had, with his pallid death-like features and burning eyes. One who reminded him of . . . he swallowed. It was a childhood fear that had momentarily surfaced to haunt him again, an illusion from a long forgotten volume of folklore and mythology, an awesome artist's impression of . . . *Satan!*

Kosminski forced himself to look agin, shied from the prospect of meeting those terrible eyes a second time, but the jostling crowd had swallowed up that terrible apparition. Somehow Premier Kosminski succeeded in convincing himself that it was just a combination of the heat and the wine he had consumed over lunch. He had nothing to fear, he had been assured of maximum protection at all times.

And, in any case, an atheist believed neither in God nor the Antichrist.

CHAPTER SEVEN

Detective-Inspector Tim Walters retired to his room after dinner. In a way you were made to feel like one of the hotel servants; you accompanied your charge whenever he went on official engagements, became part of his entourage, but the moment the razzamatazz was over you were relegated to a back seat role. Still on duty, of course, but you ate in separate quarters, were made to feel inferior to those whom you guarded. Which, he reflected wryly, was only to be expected. Damn it all, he was used to it, he had been on dozens of such assignments. Kosminski was no different from any other foreign dignitary. At least, as far as security was concerned.

You learned not to get personally involved, you were impartial, divorced yourself from political and international issues, became a classless automaton programmed to protect the life of the one you guarded, even to the extent of throwing your own body in the way of an assassin's bullet, if necessary.

It was a job, one that had to be executed with maximum professionalism and efficiency, you dared not think of it in any other way. Only a tiny majority of policemen made it to this level, you were unique in that you issued instructions to officers of a higher rank than yourself in provincial forces, and they obeyed you. You learned to strike a balance. If you deliberately threw your weight about then you were likely to find yourself on the demotion list. You lost your identity, your personality, jettisoned everything that made up an individual, so that you blended into the background and became insignificant. It was a talent, your training only complemented it. You lived by the gun and hoped that you never had to use it, but if the occasion arose your .38 was an extension of your own body, your reactions instinctive. In effect, you were a beast of prey, leashed until you were needed.

You adopted your own procedures, ensured that they did not become a routine because then you might just get careless. You sussed out the local police chief, sifted all the relevant information, garbaged the rest. Premier Kosminski had to be protected from one who was probably the best assassin in the world, the only priority. All that crap about Gospels, hippies and Antichrists could be dismissed as pure fantasy; they did not enter into this issue, they were merely distractions that might cost your charge or yourself dearly. Forget 'em.

Walters had mapped out the grounds of this country house hotel on the fringe of the city limits. He had familiarized himself with its boundaries, the hedges that would no more prevent a killer from gaining entrance than they would stop a rabbit intent upon scratching up the flower beds. Extensive lawns and a semi-circular driveway, an entrance and an exit. Vulnerable. Whoever had chosen this place as Kosminski's temporary residence had a distinct lack of forethought. If Gardener was to blame then he was due for early retirement, he was a liability. The decision should have been made by Scotland Yard. But it was too late now, Walters had to make the best of a bad job.

There were two officers stationed in the grounds, West Midlands Firearms Team officers who were doing a good job under difficult circumstances, you could not ask more of them. Guard dogs and alarm systems were there to back them up. In theory, nobody should be able to get through so Walters was superfluous to requirements, a back-up man who would not be needed. In practice, it would not be like that at all.

The officers outside in the grounds were not trained up to this kind of level, Walters mentally, meticulously, pinpointed the weaknesses. Segregate the loopholes first, then he knew what he had to do. Adopt the mentality of an assassin, figure out how *you* would kill Kosminski.

Getting past the armed guards and the dogs presented few problems. You came in from the eastern boundary so that the prevailing westerly breeze did not carry your scent to the Alsatians. The marksmen knew this and were concentrating on that side, so there were slight odds in favour of a western point of entrance. Gravel was tricky to cross and you avoided tracts of open ground, so you hugged the shrubbery until you came to the rear of the building. There was an officer positioned on the flat garage roof, so you took him out silently. No problem, a lightning strike, and you entered the hotel right there, because there was now a breach in the defence system. Disconnecting the alarm circuit was child's play, a routine procedure. And from that moment on it was Tim Walters' problem.

It might not happen like that, it might not happen at all. But that was the major flaw in the set-up so you covered it, moved on to number two. A seemingly bona-fide caller; he would pass the test because they were dealing with the best man in the business.

Number three: Walters tensed just thinking about it. The assassin might already be inside the hotel, a plant. He had personally checked out the staff list, anybody engaged since Kosminski's suite was booked was a suspect. That left just two part-time barmaids. Local girls, one married and having an affair, the other two-timing her boyfriend. Walters had a file on all four guys.

Reasons for killing Kosminski: the obvious ones were retribution for the Gdansk shootings, and creating an international embarrassment, thereby damaging *glasnost*. Plot and counter-plot; here you had to adopt a Soviet mind, confuse yourself. You did not try to keep it simple because it was far from simple. You could not rule out the fanatical element, the Nazi factor. Kosminski's uncle was reputed to have served under Himmler and Walters' research could neither prove nor disprove that, just as there was no evidence to support the belief that the premier's relative was buried in the Commonwealth Cemetery. But fanatics did not stick to facts, they often went overboard on supposition, indoctrinated themselves with it.

Finally, the assassin himself. Whichever regime was behind the plot, they would hire the best man available. Maybe even a kamikaze killer. The latter denoted a third world involvement and for the moment Walters was dismissing that. He had compiled a list of possibles and probables from the Interpol file. By a process of elimination he had reduced it to one man.

Jean Bourgoin. Nationality: French. Wanted for interrogation over three bombings, two failed assassination attempts, one success. Nickname: *The Wolf*.

If they were up against Bourgoin then the whole affair took on a different complex. Which was why Tim Walters had no doubt that the Frenchman would make it inside the hotel somehow, either by one of the methods listed or by one so far not contemplated.

Kosminski's own bodyguards would sleep on the landing. The Yard man's task was to patrol the rest of the house and, in the light of his theories, that was a tall order. He checked his watch; he had another three hours before he need start to worry. A kind of relaxation period, if there was such a thing. Time to himself, and that was something he hated because he got round to personal thoughts and they were painful.

He had come to hate himself these last twelve months. For what he had done to Jan. And he had long given up blaming the Force for what it had done to him.

Tim had never wanted to be a policeman, his application had been submitted merely to satisfy the DHSS; one could not sit around indefinitely on one's backside and draw the dole, you had to be seen to be trying to get a job. The bank and the building society had turned him down, but he wasn't worried about that because he didn't fancy an office job. He had considered the armed forces, left them in his mental pending file. Maybe if he had not nurtured a teenage gun hobby then the police force wouldn't have been so bad. Guns were the root of his problems. God, how he loathed them now!

Since his sixteenth birthday guns had become a single-minded hobby with him. It was on that farm holiday where it had all begun, the ratting foray round the outbuildings. The farmer's son had let him have a shot with a single-barrelled .410 pistol. The terriers had bolted a big rat, driven it from the pigsty into the yard, a scurrying, repulsive creature. Tim had not taken his aim, just thrown the gun up and fired, and the rodent had rolled over, its head a bloody mulch. Tim was the most surprised of everybody in that youthful gathering, but after the initial bout of euphoria had passed, he realized that, in a matter of seconds, he had mastered an art which many persevere with for a lifetime - the knack of hitting a moving target, killing it outright. Fair enough, it was scattershot, not a single bullet, but Tim Walters knew how he had achieved this feat - he had not attempted to draw a bead on it, had not poked and wavered, he had simply swung with his target and pressed the trigger at the precise moment. A knack, a talent, he knew he could do it again. And again.

A month later he joined the pistol club. Again success came easily, target shooting presented no problems for him. That year he went to Bisley with the club team and they won the shield. Somehow his hobby spilled over into his new career; only a handful of officers made it as a marksman. Tim was one of those. He was promoted to Scotland Yard's PT 17 firearms unit, the Blue Berets.

His marriage had lasted less than two years. One night Jan told him that she had fallen in love with somebody else, it was just one of those things. He understood now, when it was too late.

The siege had been the final breaking point for her. A guy made a clumsy attempt at robbing a sub post-office on a housing estate. It went wrong for him and he fled in panic, firing his sawn-off shotgun into a crowd of bystanders and killing a twelve-year-old girl. Tim got the call and was on the scene within minutes.

The bandit had forced his way into a council house, held an elderly couple hostage. A powder keg situation but the super thought they could talk it through; it was going to be a long, drawn-out business.

The road was sealed off, there were police

marksmen on the roof opposite. Then a television crew arrived and Tim remembered thinking at the time that this was one siege which Jan was going to have to go through with him.

It lasted until the afternoon of the second day, during which time Tim Walters never came off duty. At one point it seemed as if the man was going to surrender and then, without warning, a shot rang out. A body was thrown out of the front door on to the porch. It was the pensioner's. And they could hear his widow screaming hysterically indoors.

Jan would be watching every move.

The time for talking was over, it had already cost one life. Somebody had to go in there. Fast. Tim had never considered that it would be anybody other than himself; the super just nodded, a volunteer let you off the decision-making hook.

Professionally, it looked good on the play-back of the video afterwards; Tim used the low garden wall as a shield, vaulted it, rolled so that the shotblast from the broken downstairs window missed him by a yard. The guy should have practised on bolting rats.

Tim saw the killer framed in the window, reloading the single-barrel 12-gauge. Maybe he could have got to him before the cartridge was pushed into the breech, that was something that had bothered him afterwards. At the time he did not hesitate, fired instinctively, and the .38 slug mashed the bearded features to scarlet pulp.

He gained a medal and lost his wife on the same day. His reaction was to throw himself headlong into his work, a devotion which had earned him promotion; he became an inspector within two years and a top trouble-shooter after the Broadwater riots. Which was why he was here in the Midlands now, despised himself as much as he hated the .38 Smith &

Wesson which he could use with that same devastating skill if the need arose.

Relaxation periods, you were never off-duty, brought it all back. Sometimes it was the face at the window, going all over it again yard by yard, working out whether or not he could have got to the gunman in time. Other times it was Jan, wondering what she looked like now, where she was, if her new man was treating her right. Because Tim hadn't and, like the siege, there was no second chance to put things right.

With an effort he threw off his fit of melancholy. He could not afford to be distracted; Kosminski's life, his own for that matter, rested on quick thinking and instinctive shooting. Maybe afterwards he would come to a decision, but right now he was a one hundred per cent professional.

He told himself that it was The Wolf. That way he was prepared for any eventuality, a top level opponent by whose standards all the other suspects became second rate. If you could thwart Bourgoin, the rest were no problem.

Yet again he went through the file in his ordered mind, flicking through it until he came to the Interpol photograph. Not that that was much help, it was two years old, blown up to an enlargement that made it blurred and indistinct. If you thought about it, studied it, you saw the animal in the man, the narrow, cruel features, the small eyes, even the ears were pointed. But they would not be that way any more, for sure. Surgery, maybe a growth of facial hair, enough weight added to the body to fill out those lean cheeks without depriving their owner of the supreme fitness which had aided him on previous assignments. Two years . . . experience that made him more cunning, more wary. And more dangerous.

Detective-Inspector Tim Walters stepped out into

the corridor, closed the door softly behind him. On the landing above he could hear the two bodyguards conversing in their guttural native tongue. From downstairs came the clink of glasses being washed in the bar sink, one of the barmaids giggling. An atmosphere of mundanity, of normality.

He embarked upon his own process of preparation, so necessary to his attitude of mind. Standing in the darkness of the stairway shadow he forced himself to see a silhouette, one that was featureless but without any doubt the man he needed to see. Concentrating upon it, a cut-out target on the shooting-range; judging distance, picking his mark. Until mentally and physically he was prepared for the coming of The Wolf. Only then did he set off on his silent, planned tour of the hotel, pausing to listen to every sound until he had identified it to his satisfaction. For Detective-Inspector Walters had no intention of becoming the prey of the hunter.

Only once did a rogue thought fleetingly penetrate his concentration, was dismissed as swiftly as it had come; a subconscious train of thinking that stemmed from Gardener, the chief superintendent's involvement with irrelevant factors: the hippies, the Gospels, the Antichrist.

Walters laughed his contempt silently in order to speed these distractions into oblivion. If there was such a being as the Antichrist, then the nearest pretender was The Wolf, a living personification of the epitome of evil.

His straying thoughts completed their meandering cycle, and returned to their priority: The Wolf.

CHAPTER EIGHT

Prebendary Dawson had been rising regularly at six o'clock every morning during Festival week. This was in no way related to his cathedral duties, nor to the Festival itself, but simply that Scruff, his Yorkshire terrier, needed to be exercised before the visitors began infiltrating the Close. Scruff had a nervous disposition, he either cowered or refused to move, or else fled home at the sight of strangers.

A daily walk around the perimeter of the Close would have sufficed for such a small dog; indeed, it had for the first month after Dawson's arrival to take up his new post at the cathedral, and then the dean had tactfully told him that there had been complaints about canine foulings on the lawns. The prebendary had no doubt that the complaints came from his superior and not from fellow residents; the fact that other dogs were equally, if not more, to blame than Scruff was immaterial. Walkies were no longer permissible in the precincts of the cathedral, so the obvious alternative was Stowe Pool. Not a complete circuit, that was a round trip of at least a mile from Dawson's home and far too tiring for a small dog; he followed the cinder path as far as St Chad's Church and then retraced his steps. That was adequate for both of them, and thank goodness the Festival had been blessed with fine weather. When the celebrations were over he would use Beacon Park, but at the moment there were too many activities going on there.

Herbert Dawson was in his late fifties. Tall and lean, he walked with a permanent stoop, was rarely seen without his stubby blackened briar pipe clenched between his dentures, and his arrival was heralded by an aromatic cloud of broad-cut latakia tobacco mixture. He consumed an ounce a day, and when he felt that he was smoking too heavily he consoled himself with the reminder that modern packaging of his favourite brand was regulated to 25gram polythene pouches, so in real terms he had cut down since metric measures were introduced. And, anyway, an ageing bachelor was entitled to one small vice, wasn't he? Smoking wasn't like womanizing or gambling, nothing sinful. And if it was harmful then the only person he harmed was himself; this 'passive smoking' business was a lot of nonsense put about by faddy folks whose greatest delight lay in attempting to spoil somebody else's pleasure. The 'ban-everything' brigade. And *that* was sinful, certainly.

A southerner by birth, he had lived most of his life in the Home Counties, the last ten years being spent as vicar of a large parish from which he had hoped to retire. But the pressures had been too great on him, and the strain had resulted in a heart attack. Only a mild one, thankfully, and he had been prepared to resume his duties, but the bishop had suggested that he might find a prebendal appointment less stressful. And it was, in fact, a promotion. More of a sideways move, Herbert thought, but he really did not have much say in the matter. If he turned it down, then in surreptitious spite they would find him a curate's post in some out of the way village and with maybe a cut in salary to go with it. So, in the long run, it was preferable to accept the new job and take life just a little more casually. And what better way to begin the day than by exercising Scruff, but hopefully not at 6 a.m. after the Festival had closed.

Stowe Pool was an enthralling sight with the early morning sunlight scintillating on it, more of a lake than a pool, a flotilla of mallards quacking their way towards the bank in the hope of an early breakfast. Scruff bounded on ahead, turned to bark his impatience at the slowness of his master's step.

Dawson paused to refill and light his pipe, weathered a spasm of coughing before he got it going to his satisfaction. The dog had run on another ten or fifteen yards, was yapping at something at the water's edge now. Stupid animal, he was trying to frighten the ducks or, more to the point, *he* was scared of them and this was a show of bravado.

Herbert waited whilst he got his breath back. Such a magnificent setting, it was scandalous that they had ruined all but the northern side of the pool with sprawling housing estates and factory sites. He tried to envisage it as it once must have been, fields with hedges and woodland, just the odd house. Later that morning he had cause to visit the library, he would turn up an old guide book, there was sure to be a photograph of Stowe Pool and its surrounding landscape in it. He would be interested to compare the picture with his own mental impression of how this place had once been. At least in those days there would not have been all this unsightly litter on the path, that was the curse of this modern generation; today's youth had no pride in their country, they turned it into a dustbin!

Drat it, Scruff was still barking, yelping below the bank now, temporarily screened from his owner's view. The animal was incredibly stupid. Herbert knew that it wasn't the mallards exciting the dog, because they were swimming away now that they had ascertained that there wasn't any food forthcoming. The cause of the trouble was something quite ridiculous, like the other day when Scruff had worked himself up into a frenzy over a worm that was crawling across the garden path!

The prebendary clamped hard on the stem of his pipe, began to walk towards the scene of the commotion. The terrier's behaviour was most irritating; when one had made the effort to get up at an unearthly hour, solely for the dog's benefit, it then repaid you by acting in a quite irrational way.

'Oh, Lord!' Dawson stopped, instinctively recoiled and averted his gaze in acute embarrassment, gave way to a paroxysm of coughing. The pipe fell from his mouth, bounced and rolled on the path. For he had seen the object of Scruff's uncontrollable excitement and it had given him a most frightful shock, one that totally disrupted the equilibrium of a confirmed bachelor and self-confessed celibate. *For down there in the water, right up against the bank, a naked girl was swimming!*

'Scruff!' The command came out as a high-pitched squeak. 'Scruff, come here at once!'

The dog did not obey. If anything, its frantic barking escalated to an even greater frenzy. Herbert heard a splash, he dared not look back, prayed that his worse fear was not confirmed and that the dog had not leapt into the water. For, in spite of its timidity, the terrier's temperament was sometimes unreliable; last Christmas, it had attacked a relief postman and only an ill-afforded fiver had prevented the matter from going any further.

All the same, it was a sign of the times, an example of modern promiscuity, that this girl, whoever she was, had had the affrontery to bathe in a public place without even a bikini. Herbert blushed again at the memory of those bare buttocks bobbing just above the water level.

'*Scruff, will you come here, this very minute!*' A shriek of desperation, turning his back in case he inadvertently caught a second glimpse of the nude bather.

He did not really expect Scruff to come bounding back up the bank towards him, the creature was most infuriating when it got in one of its silly moods. He walked away a couple of yards, still hoped, prayed, that Scruff would follow him.

A dilemma, it made him feel quite ill, was surely injurious to his heart condition. He could not leave the girl, in spite of her brazenness, at the mercy of the dog.

'I say . . . excuse me!' A croak that was addressed to the unknown bather. 'Just splash at him, shout at him, he'll go away then.'

There was no reply, and Scruff's excited barking had now turned to a series of threatening, throaty growls. Exactly the way it had been that frosty morning when the dog had attacked that unfortunate postman. And Prebendary Dawson accepted that the only way he was going to get Scruff back was by going to fetch him, perhaps wading up to the knees in the water and grabbing hold of the snarling animal. That, in itself, was nothing when compared with the prospect of confronting a female who resembled Eve in the Garden of Eden.

He walked forward, his head turned to one side. Perhaps when Scruff saw him coming the dog would return. That, again, was a futile hope. Out of the corner of his eye he saw the dog treading water and pawing at the girl at the same time, making waves and swamping her.

'I . . . I'm most frightfully sorry . . . miss.' Dawson had an arm upraised as though to ward off an attacker, peered beneath it, was aware how his temples throbbed. 'Scruff, will you . . . '

In that instant, his embarrassment merged into shock, he jerked his eyes away, told himself that he had made a terrible mistake. A lot of swimmers floated face downwards. Except that there was something decidedly unnatural about the girl in the water, the way her outstretched arms were immobile, her legs floated lifelessly.

He dared not look again. He had to! He peeped beneath the crook of his upraised elbow, saw how the dog was scrabbling at her, slowly turning her over on to her back, righting her as a flotilla of tugs might have rescued a water-logged steamship.

Prebendary Dawson tried to scream, a shriek of sheer terror that came out as a husky wheeze. This time he was powerless to look away, was compelled to watch as that shapely body came into full view, staining the water a pink that was deepening to crimson as it moved. He saw the wound, a jagged abdominal incision that wept scarlet, followed it with his frightened eyes between the small, firm breasts until the gashed and gaping throat smiled up at him.

He just stood there, mouthing incomprehensible illogical reasons why the mutilated body in the pool was not dead. And at the very height of his terror, before his gangly legs buckled beneath him and spilled him in a heap on the cinder track, he was shouting a warning to the sleeping conurbation around him that Jack the Ripper was at large, and that the Antichrist had come as they had been warned he would.

'*This* is all we need right now!' Chief Superintendent Clive Gardener would have buried his face in his hands in abject despair had he been alone in his office.

But he had not had a minute's privacy from that moment, at 7.45 this morning, when Detective-Sergeant Griffin had phoned to say that a mutilated corpse had been found in Stowe Pool.

It was now mid-day, the Scene-of-Crime lads were still up at the pool, Gardener seemed to have been on the telephone incessantly, the only interlude being a press conference. Not just the *Mercury* and the *Herald*, some of the sensational tabloid dailies had already arrived in the city. He had had to make an official statement, just the bare facts. Literally: Name: Sharon Vaughan. Age: twenty-four. Known prostitute, two convictions for soliciting and one for shop-lifting. She had been slashed with a sharp instrument, probably a hobby knife (no, we haven't found the weapon yet, it's probably at the bottom of the pool), and at the moment we have no clues as to her attacker's identity. Motive: you can come up with all the suppositions you like but we have absolutely no idea. Yet. That's it, chaps, ten-thirty tomorrow morning and we may well have some news for you.

Of course, the sensational press were going to leap on the Jack the Ripper bandwagon; some of them were already writing their lead articles. They had not been slow to hint that the Antichrist might actually have arrived as anonymously predicted. Merge the two and evil had its price on the news stands. Political embarrassment was a best seller, too. These leeches weren't interested in facts alone, mutilations were commonplace, they could find one a week. They wanted their big story on the presses before anything cropped up to confound it. It was front page stuff for the next three days, and after that it didn't matter because maybe the assassin would have got Kosminski by then; this was the forerunner of the vultures' feast, an appetizer.

It wasn't anything to do with Detective-Inspector Walters, none of his damned business, so what the hell did he want? His job was guarding the Polish premier as well as trying to sniff out some tinpot assassin; murder was a routine matter for the local force. Gardener closed his eyes, sighed. I have a Festival to police, a peace convoy on the Chase suspected of being involved in satanic rites and perhaps intending to damage or steal the Lichfield Gospels, and in my spare time I have to set up an incident room and organize a hunt for a crazed killer. And, no, he isn't Jack the Ripper's great nephew carrying on the good work, nor is he the bishop's Antichrist. He's just a psychopath who has to be found before he kills again. Gardener looked across at the Yard man, said 'Yes?'

'I came to request an extra couple of men up at the hotel. Four aren't enough to cover the grounds properly, even six will be stretched.'

Gardener closed his eyes a second time, he sensed a headache coming on, opened them again. 'I'm sorry, I don't have a man to spare. I've already had to take six off the streets. We've had a murder, you know.' Maybe Walters didn't know because he didn't concern himself with anything less than international criminals. Police snobbery.

Walters nodded, he understood but that was no consolation to himself. Nobody missed a dead whore, they wouldn't miss a second if there was one, but one dead Pole would create an international incident with far-reaching consequences. Heads would roll, jobs would go, you had to get your priorities right. The AC wouldn't deploy manpower, Walters was expected to organize any reinforcements he needed locally; *request* them, he wasn't sure if he could demand them. He might have to push his luck, risk a backlash from Whitehall if it went wrong.

'Every woman in the city will be at risk after dark until we nail this guy.' Gardener knew what the other was thinking, had to put his case as strongly as he could. Offhand, he did not know the extent of Walters' authority in relation to local police forces; he didn't have the mental energy right now to test it. 'On a normal week it would be bad enough, on Festival week it's frightening. I've seen the body, I hope I never have to look at another one like that. Of course, the lurid tabloids will go for sensationalism, the Ripper connection with Kosminski. They might even link it to the hippies' summer solstice rites, label it a black magic ritual killing, human sacrifice and all that crap. Then they'll throw in this Antichrist bit for good measure. And miss the point altogether.'

'I can vouch for Kosminski.' Walters smiled wanly. 'He retired at 11.30, emerged at 7.20. Two bodyguards outside his door throughout the night, four police officers patrolling the grounds. Me, I just kept an eye on everybody.'

'Of course,' Gardener waved a deprecating hand, 'I wouldn't give these fanciful rumours more than a passing thought, but the media have gone to town on Jack the Ripper and the Antichrist, and it could be that some maniac has deliberately chosen his moment, the sickest joke on record. Whatever, whoever, we have to find him. With the city packed to capacity and the force at full stretch, he could have a field day before we get him. I'm sure you understand my problems.'

'I'll try to manage on what we've got,' Walters answered, 'but if anything should go wrong then maybe you and I could go half shares on a market stall or any other enterprise we might think up between us, because nothing's so goddamned certain as we'll be out with a boot up the arse to help us on our way. But I get the feeling that if anything's going to happen, it won't happen at the hotel. No, the guy we think it might be will go for something much more spectacular, he'll want to do it in front of a full house. We have to watch the visits to the cemetery and the memorial very carefully. Putting on my assassin's hat, I'd go for one or the other of those, a fitting place of execution.'

'I think maybe you're right.' Gardener was too tired to speculate. 'Of course, I'll be delegating additional men for those two places, the Firearms Team will help out, too. There'll be marksmen positioned soon after daylight, every blade of grass and tuft of heather within a mile will be searched. But we still have to let the crowds in, just as we can't stop them coming to the Festival finale. They'll be kept back, though, and there'll be no car parking within half a mile of each side of the entrance.'

'We can only do our best.' The Yard man seemed strangely sympathetic for once, perhaps he was tired, too, after his night shift. He stood up, moved towards the door. 'But our best won't be good enough if anything goes wrong. Tell you what, though, I get the feeling that whoever's hunting Kosminski is building this whole thing up to a grand finale, playing on everything that's been in the Press. No, maybe we won't dismiss the Ripper and Antichrist connections altogether, they could all be part of his publicity ploy. Just a gut feeling. Maybe I'm getting fanciful.'

And after Walters had left, Clive Gardener experienced those twinges in his stomach again, griping discomfort that could have been a touch of trapped wind. A kind of warning sign.

He told himself that he was getting fanciful, too.

CHAPTER NINE

It was with no small amount of concern that Penny realized, towards mid-morning, that Benjamin was nowhere around the campsite. At first she thought that perhaps he had wandered down to the stream or else gone for a walk in the forest, he liked to be alone when he was depressed or angry. It had happened on previous occasions after a police raid, he went off somewhere to brood and when he returned several hours later he had got it all out of his system; it was some kind of therapy which was only possible away from the proximity of others. It was futile to go looking for him, she just had to sit around until he showed up. It wasn't so much that she was worried about the hippy leader himself, but rather what he might be doing right now.

The confrontation with Haggard had riled Benjamin. Unless you knew the latter intimately you probably would not be aware of the simmering, controlled inner fury. A subversive sulk that was far more dangerous than any show of anger. The two men did not trust each other, there was a veiled feud building up between them, a mutual hatred that transcended any designs which either might have had on the Lichfield Gospels; that was merely the flash-point, there would have been one, anyway. It was as if, Penny decided, the stranger had challenged Benjamin's authority, thrown down a gauntlet. Two opposite poles, a clash of personalities that might boil up into something terrible.

Haggard was the unknown factor, one had the feeling that he was a kind of slow burning fuse that had been lit the moment he joined the hippy cavalcade. She shivered in the warm sunlight, let her eyes roam the encampment, searching for something. Not Benjamin; a kind of premonition, a niggling feeling that something was wrong and, whatever it was, it was staring her in the face yet she was unable to see it. Watching the others, a group of about thirty, making new banners to replace those which the police had confiscated: KOSMINSKI THE RIPPER.

Penny was tense, her skin was prickling, her fingernails were gouging her palms and she felt slightly sick. Oh, God, what is it, what's wrong?

And then she knew, a moment of awful realization which brought with it a surge of panic. *Haggard, the man who wore the black fedora, was also missing from the camp.*

She knew that he wasn't on the bus, there was no sign of him anywhere else. Okay, he could have gone down to the stream, or into the forest. To look for deer. She knew he hadn't, just as she knew that Benjamin had not gone for a walk just to pass the time.

A moment of awful indecision during which she fought to get herself back under control. Then she stood up shakily; there was something which she had to check on.

She reached the bus, turned and looked guiltily back towards the others. But they had not so much as glanced in her direction, they didn't give a damn whether Benjamin or Haggard were in the camp or not.

Penny closed her eyes, grasped the handrail because she felt dizzy. I don't want to look.

You have to.

The bag was there on the seat, sitting diagonally across the ripped pseudo-leather upholstery as though it had not been touched since the time she had sneaked a look inside it. It was grey with a zig-zag stripe across it, a sports bag to which a canvas shoulder strap had been attached, an improvised rucksack. Tatty, insignificant. Until you looked inside it.

She held on to the seat, wanted to retrace her steps, go back outside, tried to tell herself that Haggard's bag had not been opened since she herself had last run the zip and recoiled in horror as she viewed the contents. It will be exactly the same as it was before, there's no point in opening it again.

You have to look.

Her fingers were shaking, she could barely grasp the fastener. Sweat ran down her forehead, made her eyes smart. She was on the point of throwing up.

The zip snagged, jammed. She tugged hard and it ran with an unexpectedness that almost threw her off-balance. Her eyes were averted, stinging and blurring her vision as she stared down the littered aisle towards the gloomy rear of the bus. So hot in here, she might faint . . . and be spared the ordeal.

She forced her head round and downwards in stages, bracing herself, peering through half-closed lids and waiting for her eyesight to adjust to the semi-darkness. She saw the folded shirt, the dark material of the garment; shying from it, trying to will that black shiny snub-nosed shape to be lying there in its own hollow where it should have been.

But there was nothing on top of the shirt! Nor below it. Her trembling hands scrabbled the contents of the bag in blind panic. Stepping back, crying her fear aloud because the gun was gone.

As were Haggard and Benjamin.

* * *

Haggard walked into the city around noon, took a short-cut across the expanse of litter-strewn grass when he reached the clock tower. There was a traffic jam around the island, the queue stretching as far as the Friary traffic lights. All the car parks were full, a policeman was directing the stream of traffic down towards the railway station, causing another snarl-up at the second set of lights. From thereon the motorists had a choice of three directions, drive on, park outside the city centre and walk all the way back.

Haggard pulled the brim of his hat down to shade his eyes from the glare of the mid-day sun, headed in the direction of the parkland from which distant strains of music reached his ears. A fairground; he saw the roundabouts, the stalls, a milling throng, mingled with the crowds. Nobody spared him a second glance because his attire was somewhat drab against the background of gaudy costumes and outrageous headgear.

He paused before a shooting gallery, paid his 40p and loaded the obsolete .177.

'Five shots, forty pence,' the dishevelled youth spoke in a tired monotone. 'Five ducks and you win a prize off the top shelf.' He stood back, did not even bother to watch.

Haggard loaded, fired with a casualness that bordered on laziness. The spring grated, thirsty for oil, the compression sounded tired. Shooting and reloading with that same nonchalance, the waisted pellets striking each silhouette with just enough force to tip them over. Four down, he took an extra second to make sure of the fifth, the target unbalanced by the spent force of the slug, reluctantly going down.

Then he was sauntering on, popping the ring on

the can of tepid shandy which he could have bought for the same price on the adjacent stall without gambling his money.

His posture was one of relaxed indifference, a day visitor who neither knew nor cared about the heritage of these festivities, one who would idle away the daytime hours, drink his way through the nocturnal ones and probably sleep rough in the park with the stragglers. Yet his dark eyes flickered from side to side, missed nothing, a cine film that recorded the face of every passer-by in his brain, to be re-run later in slow motion and studied in detail.

Only once did he check his walk, alter course so that a stream of bodies swallowed him up, hid him from the oncomers. He tensed within himself, stole a glance at the red-bearded man who passed within a yard of him, clicked his tongue faintly in disappointment when he saw that the other was a stranger to him.

He crossed the road, heard the ducks on the smaller of the two lakes quacking for left-over hotdogs and sandwich crusts, followed the flow of human traffic past the memorial garden and up into the Close.

A large crowd had gathered on the west lawn of the cathedral, only a trickle filing down the wide walkway to the entrance door. Some kind of play was being enacted in the open, Haggard stood on the balls of his feet to enable him to see over those in front of him. He recognized the costumes of the actors, the uniformed and helmeted soldiers, the finery of the Royalists. He noted the muskets, the cannons in the foreground, a bulky figure in a plush cassock directing operations. A rehearsal. Haggard decided to wait for the grand performance, edged his way through the spectators and headed towards the cathedral doors.

* * *

David Vance had been a special constable for almost a year; August would see the anniversary of his joining the city's auxiliary police force. Slight of build with a pallid complexion and rimless spectacles, he would have been insignificant amongst those gathered in the Chapter House without his uniform.

His youthful ambition had been to join the Force, it had come as a terrible shock to him when he had been rejected on medical grounds. That was five years ago. It seemed a lifetime, but today it might have been different when there was an acute shortage of regular manpower. In the meantime he had clutched at the only straw that would moderate his catastrophic disappointment, had settled for a half loaf. A council office clerk by profession, a part-time policeman twice a week and on special occasions. He had booked a week of his annual local government leave to coincide with the Festival, had almost convinced himself that he was now a full-time guardian of the law.

He had patrolled the crowded streets with pride, had arrested a troublesome drunk who had leaned gratefully on him all the way to the police station. He had located two missing children and returned them to their distraught parents, had waved away their gratitude with false modesty. And when the mutilated corpse had been found in Stowe Pool his adrenalin had pumped at the prospect of an arrest, followed by a change of heart from the authority which had rejected him.

Instead, he had been taken off the beat and given the task of guarding the St Chad Gospels. His initial disappointment was tempered by the sergeant's briefing; sergeants regarded specials, especially rookie constables, as an inferior breed, they gave them the dirty work and deprived them of any credit ensuing. At least, that was how it had always seemed to David

Vance up until yesterday afternoon, when Sergeant Archibald had called him into his office.

'Look, laddie,' there was an earnestness, almost a desperation about Archibald, 'I've got a job for you tomorrow and I'm just hoping you've got what it takes. One slip-up and you'll be on the chief super's carpet and me with you, but I don't have any choice because I've no more men to spare . . . '

David accepted that there might be an attempt either to steal or to deface the vellum pages on show. These animal-libbers went to extremes, but they surely would not try anything during the daylight hours, not with so many people about. They would be grabbed before they got as far as the door, become the victims of mob law, such was the reverence bestowed upon these Gospels by the public, it seemed.

And as for this Antichrist, David had read about the 'coming' in the papers, that was either a hoax or some kind of sick publicity stunt. The last place you would find the devil, even if he existed, was in a cathedral. So there was nothing to worry about, it was going to be a boring old job, and the sarge had just exaggerated the perils of it in an attempt to make the least important copper in the city feel that he was doing something worthwhile. Thanks a bundle, Sarge.

PC Dwight had been guarding the Gospels since the opening day of the Festival, a senior officer nearing retirement, an experienced man who had twice turned down promotion. Looking at it like that, David decided, it was a responsible job, albeit an easy one. The boredom would be the worst part, that old guy's repetitive lectures which his innumerable audiences were polite enough to pretend they were listening to.

You stood at the back, hands clasped behind your back, tried to look important. After the first couple of hours you longed to sit down on one of the chairs, but if you did that then you were seen to be relaxing your vigilance. So you tried to alleviate your boredom by scrutinizing the constant flow of visitors, but in the end they all looked much of a muchness. You turned away to yawn, walked up and down on tip-toe so that your footsteps did not echo and bring disapproving glances, or irritated coughs, from the curator. At 12.30, one of the other specials relieved you for a lunch break of 45 minutes, and again for twenty minutes at 4.30. The duty ended at 6.45, when the regular night officer took over. The routine would be unchanged for the remainder of Festival week.

By the second afternoon David Vance knew the history of the Gospels by heart. They were begun in Wales, where several inscriptions were added, Gelhi swapped it for a horse from Guyal and presented it to the church of Llandeilo Fawr in Dyfed. And so on. It was like one of those catchy tunes which you couldn't get out of your head until it almost drove you crazy.

David prayed for a diversion, some wimp of a teenager threatening to slash the vellum with a penknife, one who would scream blue murder when his arm was twisted up into a half-nelson. It would make the local papers, maybe even a mention in the nationals. 'Special Police Constable David Vance acted with courage and prevented . . . '

A tiny shiver ran up and down his spine; he found himself uneasy for no apparent reason. It was illogical, here he was in the safety and boredom of a crowded Chapter House, that voice droning on with the fifteenth lecture of the day. A strange feeling, one which defied comprehension. He shivered again but this time it was because the atmosphere seemed to have gone ten degrees colder, that voice sounded distant. As if David had been abandoned, everybody had gone elsewhere and left him here on his own. That was stupid. And yet . . . *he sensed evil in the air, an unmistakable invisible malevolence that stroked the nape of his neck with its icy fingertips. And his thoughts turned again to the rumour at which he had scoffed, the arrival of Satan in this holy city with its cathedral and its own Gospels.*

There was a crash outside the Chapter House entrance, it sounded as though somebody had slipped and fallen. A momentary silence, even the curator's recitation was halted in mid-sentence. Then, scurrying feet, people rushing somewhere, muttered voices with tones of shock and anguish.

Vance did not hesitate, three strides took him to the entrance. He saw somebody lying on the flags, a pair of scuffed sneakers sticking out from between kneeling bodies. A woman's face was upturned, pale and frightened, her lipsticked mouth quivered when she spoke. 'A faint. At least . . . I *think* it's a faint!'

David Vance's heart skipped a beat, picked up speed to a fast thrumming. He had a secret fear, one that lurked in his subconscious, *the fear of death*! At twenty-five, he had yet to view a corpse. Even after almost a year in the special constabulary, he had somehow escaped that. A call-out to a fatal road accident, he had steeled himself on the way, perhaps after the first time it would not be too bad. This was a hurdle which he must overcome. When they arrived at the scene, stretchers were already being loaded into an ambulance, the bodies draped with blankets. No, they weren't dead, David told himself, not until a doctor certified them so. Even then, he had not actually *seen* them. And now . . .

It was a girl, she might just have been asleep. Like that woman had said, a faint. Her spotty face was not even pale, her eyes were closed. He felt for a pulse; it was beating, thank God!

'Perhaps somebody would be good enough to call an ambulance,' he addressed the watchers. Go on, one of you, bloody *move*!

'I've already passed the word on,' one of the cathedral guides said. 'My mate's phoning. We'd best not move her. If somebody's got a jumper or something, anything we can put under her head. And we'll need a coat to cover her with . . .'

David felt himself being pushed into anonymity. As usual. He hated this man for the way he had taken command, was issuing orders. The special constable was trying to think of something to say, no matter how trivial so long as it sounded authoritative. He opened his mouth to speak, had no idea what he was about to say, but in that instant a cry rang out, one of horror and anger, a half-scream that came from the now empty Chapter House and echoed eerily up to the roof. A shriek of disbelief, of despair, of sheer hopelessness; a familiar monotone voice that escalated to a shrill pitch.

David Vance moved, his feet seemed leaden, were holding him back. He was conscious that all eyes were focussed on him, that those around him were thinking, 'Go on, you're a copper. It's your job, not ours.'

The curator seemed to have shrunk, a pathetic dwarf-like figure clutching at one of the display frames, rubbing at it with gnarled arthritic fingers, a futile, panic-stricken attempt to remove the lines of bright purple aerosol paint that gave the page the appearance of a symbolic work of mystic art. Emblems that were almost uniform, would doubtless have been had their perpetrator been given time to work unhurriedly. Pentagons, circles, shapes that were meaningless to the casual observer continued from one page on to the next. And on still further.

The man was babbling incoherently, crying,

smudging the paint so that it obliterated even more of the ancient lettering. David Vance stood transfixed, his frightened and confused mind incapable of understanding. He was vaguely aware that those from outside were crowding in behind him, pushing, gasping their outraged disbelief at that which they saw. And inside the small Chapter House it was deathly cold, the evil force was not yet gone from here.

Someone spoke aloud, a voice that quavered and said what everybody else was thinking: '*The Gospels are ruined. Those are the marks of the devil on them!*'

David Vance found himself back outside. Alone, not even that guide was around to take command. It's your pigeon, copper, you're in charge. You carry the can.

He found himself looking for the girl who had fainted, searching the long, wide vestibule, peering into the gloomy corners. But long before an irate Sergeant Archibald arrived, he knew that they would never find her. Just a dim recollection, it might have been a trick of his bemused brain, of a man dressed in dark clothing, wearing a broad-brimmed hat, disappearing through the crowd which poured in at the west door like desert vultures that had scented carrion.

The devil's disciple, she who had feigned a collapse and decoyed the guardian of the Gospels from his place of vigilance, was gone. As was her master, he who had violated the holy scriptures.

The Antichrist himself, whose coming had been prophesied. Now that prophesy was truth, and he was here in human form, risen from his fiery hell and seeking to inflict death and destruction upon this cathedral and its city.

CHAPTER TEN

The final dress rehearsal was much improved, Don Devereux grudgingly admitted, but reminded the assembled players that there was still room for improvement. Of course, that was an impossibility, he was a realist, but the standard they had reached with the material available was not nearly as bad as he had feared.

Interruptions and distractions had not helped. On the previous occasion they were compelled to finish early to accommodate evensong. Today they had permission to rehearse up until seven o'clock but that damned disturbance had disrupted everything. He had seen the girl come hurrying out of the cathedral, there was nothing strange in that, she possibly had an urgent call to make. He remembered her features clearly, especially the acne, for she had pushed rudely past him. Then came the ambulance, followed within minutes by a cavalcade of police. Something was obviously amiss inside the cathedral; maybe a theft. Or a fight.

The actors had been told that they could not continue. Perhaps later, it all depended. Upon what? It was none of Devereux's business and he had no time to make it his. And if anybody asked, he had not noticed that girl.

The crowds were dispersed, more police arrived. The cathedral was temporarily closed to the public and there seemed to be a continual traffic of cloaked clergy to and from the houses in the Close. An air of disquiet prevailed, something serious had happened. Only later did he hear that the Lichfield Gospels had been vandalized, satanic markings sprayed all over them with aerosol paint. Don Devereux confessed to feeling a little uneasy; he had read in the papers about the threatened coming of the Antichrist. But that was nonsense, pure sadistic fantasy. Hooligans were to blame, there could be no other possible explanation, a sick hoax that had gone too far.

The Sealed Knot had performed to an exemplary level, on a par with their recent portayal of the Battle of Bosworth which he had watched on video. Because they were true professionals, they had no emotive bias like the local amateurs who seemed obsessed with re-writing history and altering the outcome of the Cromwellian attack upon the cathedral. The Round-head faction was far superior to the Royalists. With the exeption of Ron Borg, who was both stubborn and untalented except where weaponry was concerned.

The man was a disgrace to amateur theatrics! Devereux was appalled that any dramatic society could accept the gunsmith into its humble ranks, Borg's only redeeming feature here being that he understood antique firearms; he could load the muskets, clean them afterwards, and he had also volunteered to prime the cannons. That was where his usefulness terminated, a Parliamentary gunner whose only role was to supervise a continual barrage of musketry and cannonfire at the climax of the enact-ment. Presuming, of course, that all the weapons were in working order; there had been no opportunity to test the small arsenal, they had been expressly for-bidden to discharge the guns until the finale of the big performance. Canon Peebles had recoiled in horror at the very suggestion of the Cathedral Close reverberating to gunfire beforehand. At least the closing scenes would coincide with the fireworks display on Stowe Pool, so an extra bang or two was unlikely to make much difference.

Devereux had the distinct impression that the dean and chapter would have preferred the siege to have been enacted without the accompaniment of explosive reports. He was not accustomed to having restrictions imposed upon his talent for authenticity; without gunfire the whole affair would have been an unprecedented failure.

Ron Borg had a somewhat negative personality, Don decided. The other's prematurely greying hair aged him well beyond his forty-five years; reserved but not shy, he shunned company, in direct contrast to his association with the amateur dramatic society.

Of Maltese nationality, he had learned his trade on the continent, had worked for a time in the Baikal shotgun industry in the USSR, as an adviser, from where he had moved to the Czechoslovakian firm of Sellier & Bellot. Via Spain and Italy he had arrived in Birmingham, had set up his own business as a gunsmith to the trade, undertaking repair work on behalf of small retail gunshops who had no skilled craftsmen in their employ.

In 1987 his world had collapsed with the death of Ursula, his wife. A terminal illness, those last few weeks had taken their toll, left their mark indelibly etched on his features. It was after Ursula's death that Ron had joined the amateur dramatic society, as though he needed to adopt a personality divorced from his own, escape into an unreal world. They gave him small parts, minor roles, perhaps out of pity, and he repaid them by making stage scenery and props, became an asset to them in his own right.

A loner, he continued to live in the small bungalow near Sutton Park, shunned close friendships but had many acquaintances. He worked seven days a week to keep abreast of the mounting repair work, went abroad for a month at the end of July following his annual trade stand in Gunmaker's Row at the National Game Fair. His travels were not purely holidaying, rather visiting foreign gunmakers, gaining experience in the latest ballistic techniques.

This year he was going to Belgium, he had informed his colleagues during a short tea break in the Festival rehearsal. He planned to visit the Browning factory, he might be away for as long as six weeks; he made a passing reference to a brother-in-law, even mentioned a son, but he did not elaborate. His companions did not press him, they weren't interested, and to pursue the subject might have caused unnecessary grief to this polite but aloof man.

There was no chance of continuing the rehearsal, the police demanded that the Close be cordoned off to the public for the rest of the evening. A valuable treasure in the cathedral had been desecrated, they were seeking to interview a fair-haired girl, aged about twenty, who had collapsed in the cathedral, presumably to create a diversion whilst her companion(s) committed an act of sacrilege. They refused to link the incident with the Antichrist story but admitted that there might be a connection with an animal liberation group.

The girl was last seen running off through the crowd which had gathered to watch the rehearsal. It had been a large crowd, they had little hope of finding her.

Dusk was falling by the time Haggard returned to Cannock Chase. His dark clothing was travel-stained, his face was in shadow beneath the brim of his fedora, but his movements were as brisk as they had been when he had set out some ten hours ago. He had taken a direct route, followed narrow country lanes, taken a short cut through the thickly wooded Beaudesert Park and out through Brindley Heath. Forest paths and fire-breaks, terrain in which ramblers sometimes became lost, but he used the setting as his guide, in conjunction with the tall telephone tower, until at last he emerged on to the A34. Even then he kept to the tall pines, a shadow that flitted, stood still and blended in with the hedgerows when the headlights of oncoming vehicles threatened to illuminate him.

He was surprised to discover that no guard had been mounted on the Commonwealth Cemetery, approaching the unlocked gates with the wariness of a gazelle in lion country. But it was early yet, there was still a whole day and night to go before the Polish premier arrived with his entourage to lay a wreath of hypocrisy; far better to search the area thoroughly a few hours beforehand, and once it was proved to be safe then mount sentries to warn off trespassers.

He vaulted the low gates, landed with silent feline agility on the other side. The grass was springy beneath his step, the memorial towering eerily above him.

His eyes, already accustomed to the gloom of the woods, scanned his surroundings. A place of the dead, symmetrical rows of graves; Germans in a block on the left, a couple of rows of New Zealanders just apart from them, the bulk of their deceased comrades in the far right-hand corner; the centrepiece, close to the memorial, comprised three British tombstones, a squadron leader, a flying officer and an aircraftman. Haggard nodded to them as though acknowledging their presence here.

The whole area, he judged, was about an acre, bordered by rhododendrons and pine trees, shrubberies planted to break up the symmetry. He walked the perimeter, stopped frequently to study detail as dusk merged into darkness. It was with no small amount of surprise that he came upon the solitary grave set amidst the shrubs and heather, hidden beneath a clump of pines. He dropped to his knees, peered closely, and only then was he able to read the inscription on the headstone.

It was a Polish grave.

Haggard tensed, his mouth was dry. And then he was moving away, back over the gates and following the high hedge round to his left until he reached the car park. Tall trees on one side, heathland on the other, terrain that was capable of hiding a hundred assassins. He walked away, turned to peer back through the darkness, searched for some vantage point which might have overlooked the cemetery, but the graves of the war dead were securely encompassed by thick vegetation.

It was fully dark by the time he found the rough track leading off the main road to the Katyn Memorial. His sneakered feet kicked up dust clouds and he stifled a cough. Another car park, deep in the pines and heather, the balmy night air heavy with their scent.

He stopped to listen even though he knew there would be no sentries posted. Then he moved forward, saw the silhouette of the memorial stone on its raised platform like some secret temple of woodland worship. Again he knelt, not in reverence but so that he could read the lettering on the stone, barely visible as the darkness sought to enshroud this reminder of man's inhumanity to man.

IN MEMORIAL TO THE 14,000 MEMBERS

OF THE POLISH ARMED FORCES WHO WERE EXECUTED IN KATYN FOREST. NINETEEN HUNDRED AND FORTY. (1940).

Haggard's spine tingled, with an effort he suppressed a shudder that was both revulsion and anger. This was neither the time nor the place to become emotionally involved because emotions impaired clear thinking and fast reactions. Failure must not be contemplated.

Again, he checked on his surroundings, not easy in the darkness but daylight would have been too risky. The topmost branches of fir saplings, a dense thicket, were silhouetted against the early stars of a night sky, bracken brushed him waist high as he traversed this rectangular oasis amidst the afforestation and scrubland, oppressive, claustrophobic by its close proximity. Hiding places but no elevations, no obvious point of ambush.

Finally, he retraced his steps, shoulders bowed slightly as fatigue began to infiltrate his supple physique. Today he had called upon his reserves, both physically and mentally, now he needed to sleep in order to recharge himself. He debated the wisdom of returning to the encampment, the place had served its purpose, but it was perhaps still safest because it had become an integral part of his camouflage. Without it he might be conspicuous.

His reconnaissance had implanted a feeling of uneasiness, a doubt in his mind. Eliminations rather than possibilities, a narrowing of the field until there was nothing left. And a nagging fear that there was something which he had overlooked, a factor that had been so obvious that it had been discarded.

Somewhere up ahead of him, beyond the dense fir wood, he heard the muffled sounds of the hippy camp. And his thoughts returned to Benjamin, a giant of a man whose danger transcended his quick temper and sheer physical strength. You smelled more than his sour body odours for he exuded an aura of sheer evil that was almost tangible; one whose malevolence was akin to a fast growing contagious cancer, a plague that spread suffering and death throughout the land. One who must be destroyed so that others might be saved.

CHAPTER ELEVEN

Chief Superintendent Clive Gardener allowed himself the rare pleasure of basking, momentarily, in a feeling of triumph. A fleeting sense of smugness amongst the pressures which surrounded him, damn it, he had earned it. Bishops and chief constables *never* took the advice of their subordinates. An unprecedented exception had to be savoured.

Less than half an hour ago Gardener had drafted a letter requesting the resignation of Special Constable Vance; it had gone into Joan's typing tray, now it was screwed up in the waste paper basket.

'The Gospels that were vandalized were *facsimiles*!' he told Detective-Inspector Walters, resisting the temptation to gloat as he added, 'it appears that the bishop took my advice, after all.'

'Just as well for you *and* the bishop.' The other was unmoved, praises were not one of his indulgences. 'But that doesn't have any direct bearing on the incident, all it does is let everybody off the hook. Up until now I was sure that the Gospels and the threatened assassination attempt on Kosminski were two separate issues. Now I'm not so sure.'

'Oh?' Gardener looked surprised.

'The way I see it,' Walters continued, crossed one leg over the other, 'this was done as another attempt to discredit the Polish premier. Just as the murder was committed for the same reason, to highlight the rumour that Kosminski is descended from Jack the Ripper. This act has been perpetrated in yet another attempt to alienate the public from a cruel regime. See what happens when you invite a mass murderer to be your guest of honour, sacrilege and murder. Get me?'

'It's crazy.'

'Just as whoever killed this whore and sprayed dye all over the Gospels is crazy. Crazy enough to pretend that he's the Antichrist, and he probably believes it as well. We're dealing with a madman, a fanatic, and he's building up to the grand finale, Kosminski's assassination in front of a mass audience.'

'I've told you the good news, now here's the bad. It was the copies of the Gospels that were desecrated but now the bishop's insisting that the genuine articles go on show. He feels that he has conned the public, even if it has saved his priceless treasures, but he wants to compensate for his deception by putting the real McCoy on public display.'

'He's crazy, too.' Walters' expression was impassive.

'Just honest, at least you have to give him that. A fool, yes, but a man of high principles. But this time the Gospels will be protected by shatterproof glass, a bandit shield like they use in banks and post offices. And there will be an experienced officer on guard, not a rookie special who dashes off to help a damsel in distress. We have to go along with it, the chief says so.' And chief constables don't listen to advice from you or me. Bishops, once in a lifetime, and I've just had my turn. 'This time not even the Antichrist himself will be able to get to the Gospels!'

'The Gospels could have been used as a decoy to trap our man,' Walters' tone was scathing. 'I guess we missed our chance. Or rather *your* lot did. It's too late now, he won't risk it a second time. He's made his point, I guess, in his estimation he's been successful.'

'Tomorrow we begin the final run-in,' Clive Gardener was already wishing away the next forty-eight hours. 'The Commonwealth Cemetery, The Katyn Memorial and then the Close. Our man has got three chances to show his hand, we'll be watching like hawks, and . . . ' The intercom on the desk buzzed. 'Oh, I see. Well, divert every available man to the scene, put it down as quickly as possible.' He replaced the handset; he had looked tired before, now his features were showing the strain of sheer exhaustion, those of a man who had gone thirty-six hours without sleep. 'There's a riot in the Market Square, a bunch of hippies. We confiscated their inflammatory banners but they wasted no time making some more. Damn it, we can't camp out on Seven Springs waiting for the bloody things to come off the production line! They've draped them over Johnson's statue and some of our local skinheads have joined forces with the hippies to stop our chaps from pulling the banners down. Fighting is in full swing,' he smiled weakly, 'but we'll sort 'em out, teach the buggers a lesson!'

Walters stood up. 'I'd like to ask a favour.' There was a fleeting self-consciousness about him, he wasn't accustomed to asking favours of anybody. 'I'd like your best CID man up at the hotel tonight. I have to . . . go out.'

Gardener nodded. 'A lead?'

'Maybe. Or maybe I'm barking up the wrong tree. Just a hunch, but I reckon on a fifty per cent success rate where gut-feelings are concerned. If you could help out . . . '

'Of course.' The chief superintendent watched the

other move towards the door, Walters was damnably tired, too. Almost as tired as himself. 'And best of luck, wherever you're going.'

Tim Walters had studied the Scene-of-Crime reports in detail. He had also visited the morgue to check on Sharon Vaughan's mutilated corpse; the pathologist had still to submit his full findings. It was a routine murder enquiry, the responsibility of the local force, Walters had no authority to intervene even though he suspected it was linked to his own assignment. The Chief would probably have okayed it if he'd requested it, but there was no time to lose. It might be a false scent laid to divert the hounds. The Wolf himself might even be a red herring deliberately thrown in by the assassin, but a few hours of the Yard man's time was a calculated gamble.

Playing a hunch had a distinct advantage over conducting a methodical enquiry – you didn't play it by the rules. There were no rules, you were a free agent with a roving commission. But there had to be a starting point. This time there were three: the Commonwealth Cemetery, the Katyn Memorial and the Close. Walters visited all three, checked them out. There were no vantage points where a marksman could lie up, pick his target from a distance with a high-powered rifle. All three locations were encompassed by their various surrounds, whether it was tall pines or ecclesiastical dwellings. Which reduced the field of fire considerably, excluded the long-range ambush completely. Those admitted to the two Cannock Chase sites would be vetted, the public would be restricted to a roadside view of the approaching and departing cavalcade; and it was an all-ticket crowd for the mock siege of the cathedral. There was always the possibility that a stranger might slip through the security net. On the other hand, he might not have to go to those lengths. *Because he was already known and accepted, above suspicion.*

Vague possibilities but they were worth pursuing.

Walters made his way on foot to the Close, paused by the floodlit Minster Pool. Some youths were throwing stones into the water and the ducks were quacking their annoyance, swimming across to the opposite bank where overhanging trees offered them some protection from the missiles. A line of multi-coloured fairy lights bowed over the water, created a kaleidoscope of colours on its surface. People lined the railings, water held a fascination in any setting.

The stone throwers tired of their futile game, moved on. An empty lager can floated towards a morass of fish and chip papers, litter attracting its own kind, becalmed in a greasy scum.

Tim Walters was in no hurry; it was early yet and he had not formulated a plan of action. He was reminded of his early Metropolitan days. You were assigned to a case, an area. You went there, let events unfold around you, played them as they needed to be played. In all probability nothing would happen tonight. It would be a fruitless foray. The hairs on the back of his neck prickled, told him that it would not be so. He kept an open mind about premonitions, like hunches, he was too experienced to discard them altogether.

The pubs were turning out, he heard shouting in the municipal car park behind the high red-bricked wall that backed on to Pool Walk. There might be a fight; it was none of his business.

A hundred yards further on he turned right into the Close. The cathedral was illuminated, powerful spot-lights playing their beams on its magnificent archi-tecture like searchlights picking out enemy bombers.

People strolled on the lawns, a courting couple were necking in the shadows of the neatly trimmed shrubs which surrounded the old well. The tall house in the corner had a dozen or more lighted windows, a private school where the pupils had been privileged with an extended bedtime because of the celebrations. He glimpsed scurrying figures on the top floor, disappearing as they dived for their beds before the duty master entered. The lights were extinguished.

He should have left it another hour, he had succumbed to the over-eagerness of a plain clothes recruit, the kind who were found next morning with a knife in their back; except that this was not the sinful metropolis, it was more dangerous because one was lulled into a false sense of security. And there had already been one killing.

The night was warm, the pullover covering his T-shirt was superfluous, but for sure there would be a chill in the air later. He followed the upper boundary of the Close, glanced briefly into the driveway of the old bishop's palace which also incorporated the cathedral school. Just a couple of lights were showing, they were probably left on all night.

The path turned sharply at right angles when it reached the low sandstone wall, bordered by majestic horse chestnut trees, an avenue of deep shadow beyond the illuminations. Walters peered over the wall, stared down into the dark abyss of a sunken garden, caught the aroma of decaying vegation and stagnant dampness. To the east the sky was a fiery glow, the illuminations reflected in the still expanse of Stowe Pool as if the water was still tinged with blood. Less than forty-eight hours ago a mutilated corpse had floated on its shore. That was the starting point of his hunch.

He was strolling along the south road of the Close

when the floodlights were extinguished with startling suddenness, plunging the ancient surroundings into instant darkness through which the distant glow of the city lights slowly permeated. When he reached the chain-link barrier fence he turned back up into the Close. He had completed a circuit, a reconnaissance. The preliminaries were over.

Everybody seemed to have gone. He listened intently in case that amorous pair were still by the well, but there was no sound other than the far-off hum of the nocturnal city. On his left, parked against the kerbside, was the chunky silhouette of the lorry which he had first noticed two days ago, a maroon Bedford with a green tarpaulin roped over its shapeless load. A gust of summer breeze soughed through the tall trees, ruffled the PVC sheeting. Walters moved forward until he was hidden by the tailboard.

He had no reason to investigate, just an inquisitive intuition, his fingertips smoothing along the ropes until they came to a knot. Expertly, effortlessly, he unthreaded it, felt the tension slacken, the tarpaulin loosen. He stooped, thrust his head up into the gap and shone the beam of his miniature torch inside. Cannons! Two of them, detached from their wheels, they must have weighed in excess of a ton each at a guess, their ironwork painstakingly restored by some enthusiast so that their condition today was as good as it had been centuries ago. Primitive weapons for killing and maiming, for demolishing fine buildings which the occupants stubbornly refused to surrender. Machines of dreadful destruction.

Tim Walters reached out and touched one, shivered at the feel of its cold ornate craftsmanship. He moved his torch in an arc, looking for the cannonballs, but there were none. There wouldn't be, of course, the guns would only be firing a charge of black gunpowder, a reverberating boom and a cloud of villainous smoke to add realism to the play-acting.

That earlier premonition, a sense of awful foreboding, returned, brought with it a goosepimpling of his flesh, travelled up his spine, raised the hairs on his neck and spread into his scalp. His thoughts flitted, back to the body in the pool, the Ripper theory. And the Antichrist! He tensed, his inbuilt warning system was playing tricks on him, this cargo of antiquity had no bearing upon his investigation. He should not be here, his job was back at Kosminski's hotel trying to outwit The Wolf. The French assassin was a real threat, the rest were just fantasies.

He ducked back out into the night air, quickly reefed the knot back into place. But the feeling did not go away, continued to plague him, had him peering into the shadows cast by the nearby houses, seeing shapes that moved into a threatening nothingness.

With an effort he shrugged off the persistent uneasiness, told himself that he was wasting his time. The Chief would ball him out if ever he got to know, but he wouldn't because Tim Walters, assigned to special duties, would not include it in his report.

A covered archway led off through the buildings opposite the school house. Through it he saw a circle of streetlighting on a neatly mown lawn. He hesitated, it seemed to beckon him on just as that inexplicable warning was trying to hold him back. *Don't go!*

He moved forward out of stubbornness, cursed that Job of an instinct beneath his breath, stood in the shadows of the arch surveying the picturesque square of half-timbered fifteenth century houses set around two courts. An oasis of tranquillity hidden away from the prying eyes of tourists.

He was a trespasser, he had no business here. An

unfamiliar feeling of guilt had him starting to back away, turning to anger because subconsciously he had pandered to his imagination again. He was wasting his time, had spurned his responsibilities, even this very minute the man whose life he had been assigned to guard might be in danger from The Wolf.

Just as his own life was this very second.

Tim Walters hesitated for one fateful second, a moment in which he again dwelt on his premonition, felt it vibrate every nerve in his body. He jerked round but he was too late, the knife blade had penetrated deep between his shoulder blades, was hacking and twisting, spearing him like a gaffed fish. He attempted to cry out but only a choking gurgle escaped his lips as he sank slowly to the ground. The flagstones beneath him were as cold as gravestones, the lamplight in the courts had turned a misty crimson before his eyes.

Fleeing on all-fours, dragging himself along crablike but going nowhere, a half circle that had him looking back into the deep shadows of this centuries-old alleyway. A shape, a silhouette that was blacker than the enshrouding darkness, he sensed rather than saw it, felt its sheer malevolence as it stood there waiting for him to die. His strength had ebbed, his pistol weighed him down but he was powerless to grope for it. He heard his blood dripping, smelled it, tasted its iron flavour; coughed and spat.

The initial pain was gone, he felt weightless, thought he might float away to safety. He was back by that sandstone wall at the far end of the Close, clutching at the parapet as a wave of vertigo swept over him. Below him was a dark, bottomless abyss that went right down to hell. The domain of the Antichrist.

Tim Walters gave up the fight, allowed himself to slide gently down into the blackness.

CHAPTER TWELVE

'You bastard!' Penny's bunched knuckles took Benjamin full in the mouth, jerked his head back. He staggered off balance, sprawled across the front seat of the bus. The flickering flames of the campfire outside cast weird shadows on the ceiling, the spruce tops a company of witches wearing tall hats, assembled for a Sabbath.

'Bitch!' He made no move to get up, wiped a trickle of blood from a split lip. 'I've a bloody good mind to . . . '

'You've been with *her*!' Penny waved a hand in the direction of the gathering outside. 'That poxy whore, Diane Wilkes. Oh, God, you disgust me, don't you ever come near me again!'

'Listen . . . '

'I don't want to listen to your lies.'

'Listen, damn you!' He struggled up on to an elbow, his expression smouldering with anger and humiliation. 'I got it, Pen. Oh, Jesus, I got it and I couldn't have done it without her.'

'Got what?' Hands on hips, she regarded him contemptuously. 'There's only one thing you're likely to get from Diane Wilkes and I'm not having you passing it on to me!'

'Stupid cow!' His fingers flexed, he was having to fight to keep himself under control. And then he laughed, a deep sound that embodied both bitterness and mirth, escalated to a crazed peak. 'I got those Gospels, Pen. See!' He fumbled beneath a ragged blanket, held up an aerosol can, its cap missing. 'Purple touch-up paint for cars. I pissed it all over those pages, I tried to make a pentagon but there wasn't time, the bastards probably wouldn't recognize one if they saw one, anyway. I also drew an inverted crucifix. But I did it for those animals which were sacrificed for the hypocrisy of a do-gooder. They'll never get it off, I promise you that, they'll remember this day for the rest of their bloody lives. And d'you know what my next target is?' He lowered his voice to a throaty manic whisper.

She backed away a pace, stared at him in shocked horror. He was mad, madder than she had thought. And dangerous.

'The Mappa Mundi!' His top lip was bleeding freely but he was oblivious of both the wound and the pain.

Penny stole a glance behind her, she thought about fleeing but Benjamin would follow her, catch up with her. Even if she made it as far as the woods he would follow her scent like a beast of prey, run her down. 'Oh,' she replied weakly.

'See,' he stabbed a finger at her, 'that's why I took Diane and not you. Because you lack guts, you wouldn't have done what she did, faked a collapse so that everybody, including the pig on guard duty, went to help her. Seconds it took me, and then we were both away, lost ourselves in the crowd.' His brow furrowed. 'We split up. Is she back yet?'

'I've no idea,' Penny's voice was shaking. 'There's been some trouble, I believe. Some of the others took the banners to town, there was fighting. Almost a riot. There were arrests. If Diane's missing then she's probably cooling off in a police cell right now.' God, how I wish she was, she thought.

'No,' he looked out of the window but it was impossible to see anything except firelit silhouettes. 'No, she would have come straight back here, she wouldn't have got involved in any demonstrations. I'd better go and look for her.'

'And you can bloody well have her!' Penny backed to the door, and again her eyes were seeking out that rucksack on the third seat down the gangway. It had not been moved since she had last seen it.

'Where's Haggard?' His gaze followed her, there was sudden alarm in his tone.

'How the hell should I know? I presumed that the two of you had gone together.'

It might have been a trick of the orange fireglow but she thought that his features paled. 'He's a weirdo. I know he's up to something but if it was the Gospels, then I beat him to it. I don't want him around the camp any longer. When he shows up I'm going to tell him to get the hell out of here, and if he knows what's good for him, he'll go.'

'You do that,' she turned away, began to descend the steps. 'Do just what the hell you like with him, I don't give a sod for either of you.'

She was afraid that Benjamin might come after her, was scared to look back as she walked unsteadily across the clearing. She was still trembling, she had never believed that Benjamin would actually go for the Gospels. It had been fun talking about it, sheer bravado, but you didn't get away with anything as big as that. Abattoirs, butchers' shops, you broke in, rendered the meat inedible but the police were too busy to make more than cursory enquiries. But vandalize something worth a million quid and the heat was on. They'd find the culprit, they'd be right back here. She wasn't hanging around to wait for them. Benjamin was welcome to Diane Wilkes, the latter had done her a favour. Benjie and Di deserved each other. But right now she was going to put as much distance between herself and the campsite as possible.

The night was warm, there was enough light from the myriad of stars in the sky to see your way by; you found a track leading away through the scrubland, stayed on it, and eventually you were bound to emerge somewhere. It didn't matter where, so long as it was far away from the hippy camp. Ahead of her she could hear the trickle of running water, the wide stream where the deer came to drink after dark. She would cross it, follow that long straight path that joined the main road. Turn right, away from the city, head north.

'Hi!'

Penny started, almost cried out aloud. Directly ahead of her, barring her way, she saw the outline of a man and there was no mistaking that hat, the paleness of features that were almost luminous in shadow. Standing there in the faint starlight he seemed much taller, it might not even have been the man who called himself Haggard. But she knew it was him, remembered again how that pistol had gone missing from his bag, but even then she wasn't afraid. Because he wasn't like Benjamin, he was strong and gentle; he respected a woman. He was dangerous, all right, but not to her.

'Oh, it's *you*!' She tried to sound more surprised than she was as he moved closer to her and she was able to discern those features in the ethereal half-light. She was aware how her heart pounded and her pulses raced, still feared that Benjamin might be on her trail and his rage would be terrible if he found them here together. She thought she heard the undergrowth rustle some way back as though he pursued her, stalked her stealthily through the undergrowth, awaiting his opportunity to spring upon her. But suddenly she was no longer afraid because the stranger in the black fedora was here to protect her.

'You look like you're leaving for good, running away.' He was shrewd, or else by some magical means he was able to read her thoughts, knew already what had happened.

'Yes,' she spoke in a whisper, resisted the impulse to look behind her. 'I am. I . . . I . . . it's Benjamin, he's as crazy as a bear. Don't . . . don't go back to the camp, Haggard, because he's looking for you!' Her warning came out in a rush, an unmistakable plea.

'Why not?' He raised an eyebrow and she thought that his thin lips smiled and mocked her fear.

'Because,' a sudden surge of panic, she wanted to push past him and run whilst there was still time. 'Because . . . *Benjamin will kill you if you go back!*'

Haggard laughed softly, a sound that reminded her of the rushing brook down below, a self-assurance rather than an arrogance, the confidence of a man who walked tall and feared none. Then she remembered the gun again and shuddered. It wasn't in the bag on the seat so he must be carrying it, or had it hidden somewhere.

'I think maybe I'd better see you to some place of safety at any rate.' He stood to one side for her to join him. 'I can see that you're terrified of him catching up with you. And as you're obviously not going back to the camp, I can't leave you out here at this time of night all on your own.'

She found herself walking beside him, keeping pace with him, and even after he had helped her across the stream his arm remained around her. In the far distance she saw the headlights of speeding cars on a main road, heard the hum of engines.

'I guess we'll have to kip out in the open tonight.' He halted within a couple of hundred yards of the main road, began to steer her gently towards a silver birch coppice that was starkly outlined on a landscape of bracken and heather. 'That'll do, I suppose, then in the morning we can both go our separate ways.'

It was snug and warm in the bracken beneath the trees, a clump of heather as soft as any pillow, staring up at the twinkling stars. For the first time for a very long time, Penny felt at peace with the world. She welcomed the closeness of this stranger who had joined the convoy because he needed to travel and now, like herself, he was moving on.

Suddenly she broke the long silence, told her companion how Benjamin and Diane had penetrated the tight security in the cathedral and sprayed the Gospels. It was as though she had to purge herself, divorce herself from a plot of which she had once talked eagerly because she never suspected that anything might come of it. And now that it had, she needed to exonerate herself in her own conscience.

'You reckon he did it?'

'I *know* he did. Benjamin's a liar at times but not this time.'

'In case it's troubling you,' Haggard was whispering now, his lips close to her ear, 'I'll let you into a secret. Those weren't the real Gospels, they were copies!'

She sat up, stared incredulously, thought at first that he might be joking. Or he had made a mistake. Or was simply trying to reassure her with a lie. But when he began to laugh, she laughed with him, laughed until she was crying with sheer relief. Then she stopped as a thought struck her and she remembered that earlier confrontation between Benjamin and Haggard, and how the latter had to be carrying his gun because it was gone from the bag in the bus.

'Haggard?' His face was close to her own, his fingers squeezed hers with an exciting tenderness.

'Yes?'

'What are you really doing here?'

He paused, she heard a slight intake of breath. 'Travelling.'

'I know that you're carrying a gun.'

She felt him stiffen, his grip suddenly tightening over her fingers, and that deep breath was expelled slowly. 'You've been looking in my bag, then.'

'Yes,' and she added quickly, 'but Benjamin doesn't know, nobody does. I haven't told anybody.'

'I'm getting careless.' He relaxed his grip. 'Still, if nobody else knows, then I guess it doesn't matter. But I'm glad you're away from the camp, Penny.' It was the first time that he had called her by her name.

'What's going on, Haggard? I know that something is and I don't mean just with you.' She held her breath, awaited his reaction.

'To be absolutely truthful, I don't rightly know.' He pulled her close to him. 'There seemed to me to be a lot of people doing a lot of different things, all for different reasons, and all getting tangled up with one another. Benjamin's been after the Gospels and right now is thinking that he's hit his target. There's a prostitute been found mutilated in the city lake. There's a bunch of hippies demonstrating against the Polish prime minister, rioting and getting themselves locked up. And to enrich the mixture there's supposedly, according to the papers, a plot to assassinate the Pole, who's supposed to be a descendant of Jack the Ripper. You couldn't really blame anybody for putting a bullet between the bastard's eyes, could you, Penny?'

'No, I guess not. He's responsible for the slaughter of innocent workers whose only crime was to stand up for basic human rights. And if he *is* a relative of Jack the Ripper's, and this prostitute has been mutilated, I guess you could just jump to conclusions, couldn't you?'

'There's a rumour that the Antichrist, the devil, is going to return to Earth, turn up in Lichfield.' It was as though he was talking to himself now, speaking his thoughts aloud. 'But I guess that's just too fanciful, even more far-fetched than this Ripper theory.'

Then his lips found hers, and she trembled as he kissed her, clung to him. But there was one last question she had to ask, the only thing that troubled her now.

'Haggard, why . . . why do you carry a gun?'

'Just in case I happen to need it,' he replied, and his lips found hers again, brushed them softly and then crushed against them, preventing her from asking any more questions. His tongue, pushing its way into her willing mouth, was too busy to talk further, anyway.

And suddenly Penny didn't care whether or not Haggard carried a gun or, if he did, for what reason. Because, right or wrong, she would stick by him.

CHAPTER THIRTEEN

Chief Superintendent Clive Gardener was convinced that he was having a heart attack.

He had gone without sleep for forty-three hours; that was because of the discovery of Detective-Inspector Walters' body in Vicars Close just as Gardener was about to finish the longest spell of continuous duty in his career. The call had come through at 7.45 a.m. He had finally climbed into bed at 2.30 that afternoon, still on call if he was needed urgently.

At 5 p.m. he received a call from Whitehall, the assistant commissioner himself. Terse and to the point, no confidentiality, no explanations. This is how it is, Chief Superintendent . . .

One of our men has been murdered. We cannot presume that his killer is the man whom we believe intends to attempt to assassinate the Polish premier. Neither can we rule out that possibility. Nor can we assume that Walters' murderer is the same person who mutilated a local call girl. Right? Good. Then it is a straightforward murder enquiry, no hint to your force or the press that Walters was engaged on a special assignment. That is your line of approach but the enquiry must in no way become a priority over the safety of Premier Kosminski. Detective-Inspector Walters' replacement will be reporting to you shortly.

In the meantime, security cover is the prime responsibility of the Firearms Team.

An understandable cover-up. Gardener went through to the bathroom, showered. Straight back on duty, maybe for another thirty-six hour stretch, perhaps even until after the closing Festival ceremony, when the police escort would whisk Premier Kosminski back to his waiting plane at Birmingham International airport. Only then would Clive Gardener's awful responsibility end.

He tried not to think about the killing. Just give me another half hour, an extension of my interrupted break. He was towelling himself when he felt his pulse rate begin to speed up, his temples started pounding like distant jungle drums, becoming closer, louder, all the time. Every muscle, every nerve in his body tautened, his skin was at full stretch, it might split open at any second.

He experienced the terror of the first time cardiac arrest victim, clutched at the towel-rail, heard the fittings loosen inside the wall. Every limb in his body was shaking. Oh, God, I'm going to die!

'Are you all right, Clive?' Madge's voice, she was knocking on the door, it was sheer stupidity locking yourself in the bathroom after thirty years of marriage. She sounded a million miles away.

Panicking. Oh, Jesus Alive, why do couples still lock bathroom and toilet doors when there's nobody else in the house? Because of inhibitions surrounding natural bodily functions that transcended frankness where sexual openness was acceptable.

'*Clive*?' Madge was rattling the door knob now.

'I'm . . . all right.' He took a deep breath, fought to bring himself under control, felt his shaking start to steady. Yes, I *am* all right, it isn't what I thought it was, after all.

'Are you sure? You've been in there an awful long time.'

Perhaps he had been in the bathroom longer than he had realized, that awful sensation had lasted for minutes instead of seconds. He knew now what it was. *A panic attack*, the condition for which doctors prescribed tranquillizers, maybe addicted you. But he had beaten it. He told himself that it would not happen again now that he recognized the symptoms. 'I'll be out in a second, don't worry.'

Madge Gardener stood there on the landing, wearing her baggy green tracksuit which was intended to disguise a middle-aged weight problem, her features white and strained. 'Clive, you look dreadful!'

'I'm all right, honest.' He kissed her on the cheek. 'Just tired. I have to go back to the station.'

'Oh, *no*!' She clutched at his arm, felt how he trembled. 'You have just done the longest stint ever. You're not well enough to go on duty again right away.'

'I have to,' he scarcely recognized his own voice, a tired faraway whisper. 'That was the AC himself who phoned.'

'Then you'd better go sick!' There was a note of futile pleading in her voice because she had been married to a police officer for far too long even to hope that he might take her advice. She did not ask what the assistant commissioner had said because even chief constables' telephone calls were taboo between husband and wife.

'I'd better get dressed.' He pulled himself free of her. 'I hope I'll be home before morning.'

As he drove back towards the city he began to tremble again, but for a different reason this time. The last thing he relished right now was a meeting with the Yard's latest hit man; they were a breed apart from normal police officers, even the Firearms Team. A kind of cross between a human being and a stoat, a species trained to hunt by scent, everybody was prospective prey until proved otherwise. Subconsciously you had a lurking fear of them, whatever your rank, not just because of what they did but of what they were.

Ron Borg had snatched a quick pizza and chips before driving his Peugeot off the Minster car park. He had lapsed into the habit of eating out, the preparation of food was both time-consuming and pointless to a man alone.

The traffic was congested and it took him twenty minutes to clear the city limits, another fifteen to reach his bungalow, leaving the car outside in the road because this was only a port of call. There was a job he had to do before morning.

His spare bedroom was no longer furnished for accommodating overnight guests. On the infrequent occasion when a foreign customer visited him he booked him in at an hotel. That had become a routine procedure allied with eating out. The varnished interior door had been replaced by a steel one with double security locks, the single window fitted with a mesh grill. At the far end stood a workbench littered with specialist tools; adjacent to it, bolted to the wall, a seven-gun capacity firearms cabinet. Not impregnable, nothing was in these days of sophisticated criminals, but the burglar alarm was *almost* foolproof.

He unlocked the cabinet, removed the chain from the trigger guard of a Winchester 101 over-and-under 12-bore shotgun. He handled it appreciatively, lovingly, for a few seconds, recalled how he had worked to remove the choke on the previous day. A gun that had patterned too tightly, needed opening up to increase the shot spread for a discerning clay target marksman. The customer to whom it belonged could have traded it in part-exchange for the ready-made weapon, but to the dedicated shooter a gun was akin to a wife, you moulded your beloved to your own requirements.

At the time, Ron thought, it had seemed like sacrilege. The Winchester, in the manner of its famous ancestors, had been bored to shoot hard and tight. He had changed all that. But the theory had to be proved in practice; it needed a trial before being returned to its owner. Many gunsmiths would simply have relied on their experience, had faith in their craftsmanship; Ron Borg had both of these but he still insisted on testing his own work. He was a perfectionist. More than that, if he was honest with himself, he did not even need an excuse to go to the shooting ground, he just longed to be there, to feel the recoil of the stock against his shoulder, smell the burned powdersmoke and thrill to the satisfaction of a clay disc crumbling to dust at his shot.

'Good evening, Mister Borg.' Michael was working the traps this evening, freckled faced and smiling, a young man whose ambition was to throw clays so that they beat the best shots in the country.

'Evening, Michael.' Borg had an unaccustomed tenseness about him, was allowing it to show now that he was away from the Close and the rigmarole of Roundheads and Cavaliers. On occasions he regretted his involvement in amateur dramatics; like this evening when the daylight was going to linger as long as possible, and even after ten o'clock one would be able to smash a white target in the reluctant dusk.

'What'll it be, Mister Borg?'

'The sporting lay-out.' The other opened the breech of the Winchester, pointed the barrels skyward, scrutinized their mirrored finish for the slightest imperfection, but there was not so much as a blemish to be seen . . . 'As they come, fast and hard, fifty straight off. I need to test this beauty on everything that's going.'

Borg loaded, stood in readiness, the shotgun held waist high, not for him the clay marksman's pose before he shouted 'pull'. In his book that was an unfair advantage, you gave your quarry a start even if it was only an inanimate round object.

The 'Springing Teal' were first, a pair of targets rising steeply, fast; separating. He powdered the first, smashed the second into fragments. He seemed to relax now as he reloaded as if, hitherto, he had been unsure of his own marksmanship.

Two more of the same, this time he disintegrated both in puffs of black dust. On to the next stand, this time high targets hurtling towards him, simulating driven pheasants at a covert shoot; he took them far out, fragmented them at tree-top height. Michael tried to surprise him with a second brace, but he smashed those as cleanly as the first.

Lower ones now, partridges flushed from the clover field; he let them spin close, showered himself with their remnants. A pair broke to his right; they did not get far. Neither did the single one which followed almost instantly, almost caught him unloaded.

He missed a 'woodcock'. The trapper insisted that a miniscule flake had chipped off the disc but in Borg's book that was a miss. Now he was taking them all early, instinctive reaction shooting, no longer testing the gun but himself; the weapon in his hands was just the means of destruction, a co-ordination of mind and body, the killing machine.

Forty-eight to fifty, he insisted on a second miss, to have agreed with Michael that the 'driven grouse' had been chipped would have lowered Ron Borg's self-imposed high standards. The gun's modification was a hundred per cent success, his own performance an acceptable ninety six out of a hundred.

'Thank you, Michael.' He passed over a twenty pound note, reminded himself that it had to be added to the customer's account. 'That will do fine. I don't expect I'll see you before next Wednesday at the earliest. In the meantime I have to busy myself with flintlocks and cannons, blank charges and human targets that simulate a hit, and all that sort of thing.'

The trapper laughed. It seemed an anti-climax after a high-scoring round of clay pigeons in which the competitor would surely have won his heat handsomely in the club's monthly sporting shoot.

Don Devereux eased his Renault into the late evening flow of Festival traffic some two hours after Ron Borg's departure. He cursed the slow-moving cars, the traffic signals which were surely out of sequence, favouring the stop signal purely to infuriate the frustrated motorists.

The car had held the heat of the day long after the sun had dipped below the western horizon, the sweat poured down his thick-set features in spite of two open side windows and a raised sun roof. The actors had the easy part, he reminded himself yet again, even the accomplished Sealed Knot. They had their scripts, they only had to follow them with some degree of reality. He had to do all that as well as organize everybody else, supervise the entire proceedings. And there was always a fool, on and off the stage, more often in the plural. Stupidity extended beyond the realms of those physically involved in the performance.

The dean was still resisting the use of weaponry in the Close in spite of the bishop's agreement to the firing of blank muskets and cannons. Could not the gunfire be cut to an introductory duo of shoulder gun shots and a single, reduced powder charge, cannonade? No, it could not, unless the Stowe fireworks display was minimized to two rockets and a show of Catherine wheels and sparklers!

Of course, the attack on the facsimile Gospels had unnerved the cathedral's hierarchy, Devereux smiled one of his rare smiles, they would have cancelled the re-enactment of the siege had it been possible. Cathedral treasures, albeit copies, had been desecrated, they had no wish to be reminded of seventeenth century wanton destruction. And, there was no getting away from it, the satanic symbols sprayed on the vellum pages had them looking over their shoulders, grown men scared of their childhood bogeyman – the Antichrist! All of which made Don Devereux determined to create an atmosphere of realism on the finale night. He smiled whimsically to himself. It would be an added dimension to bring the devil in at the finish, scare the bishop and his colleagues out of their longjohns! But, in the meantime, Devereux had more urgent matters to attend to.

He had changed out of his Parliamentary finery into a pair of cords and a loose fitting cardigan. He was tense, uneasy, accelerating with an air of urgency as the outgoing traffic thinned on the A38; most of the vehicles were oncoming, city-bound, office and factory workers shedding the fatigues of the day's labours as they headed back to the Festival and the many recreations which it had to offer. Devereux was in pursuit of his own pleasures in the opposite direction.

He had familiarized himself with Birmingham during that week of the Battle of Bosworth, remembered the ring road and the streets leading off it. Artificial lighting revealed familiar landmarks, created its own cloak of furtive protection.

He slowed, watched the road behind in his rear view mirror. His mouth was dry, his hands slippery on the steering wheel. Intermittent traffic, cars turning off, others easing out into the mainstream. A near-deserted street, Victorian houses with littered pavements. His narrowed eyes searched for silhouettes in the shadows, perhaps the firefly glow of a cigarette smoked to convey a half-hidden presence.

Less than 10mph now, peering into the shadows, negotiating a badly parked car, peering furtively. The road was momentarily deserted of traffic, empty houses boarded up, graffiti sprayed on their crumbling brickwork. A faulty streetlamp gave an extended length of darkened pavement. Devereux tensed, something moved in the shadows.

His heartbeat quickened as he recognized a silhouette that was female, long hair straggling over a dark coat, a slovenliness about the way the wearer leaned up against a frontage wall, eyes that watched his car even though he was unable to see them. He felt them, the way they urged him to pull in to the side.

One last check of the mirror; there were no vehicles in sight except that solitary parked car that was, in all probability, stolen and abandoned. A moment of apprehension and guilt in which he almost accelerated and drove on; instead he braked, scuffed the kerb with his nearside tyres. Stopping, stalling the engine as his trembling foot slipped off the clutch pedal.

He sat there, perspiring heavily so that he smelled his own body odours, praying that the approaching figure would walk on by. It had all been a mistake, she was just waiting for a friend who had failed to show up, she would not approach a stranger. She would hurry on, he would follow her progress in his mirror as far as the next lamp standard, listen to the receding tip-tap of her stiletto heels until she was swallowed up by the suburban semi-darkness. Urging her to carry on walking. Don't stop! He wanted to scream abuse at her but his mouth was too dry to form the words. Fear and guilt vied with an overwhelming urge, and by the time she had clicked the handle of the passenger door he was smiling at her, heady with the odour of cheap perfumes that exuded from her as she slid into the seat beside him.

CHAPTER FOURTEEN

Penny was vaguely aware that Haggard had moved away from her. In her sleep she felt the cool night air against her where he had been, stirred restlessly but was too exhausted to waken. It had all been a dream, a wonderful, exciting figment of her subconscious. Now it was all over, she would return to reality and discover that she was all alone out here on the heathland, that her lover had gone his own way after their brief meeting outside the campsite. *If* they had ever met. In all probability she would never see him again, he had flitted briefly into her life and was gone again. A groan of dismay and disappointment escaped her lips; far better not to have dreamed than . . .

'You okay, Pen?'

She started, came awake instantly, trembling. Against the fading stars she saw him, a tall silhouette with that hat at a rakish angle, buttoning his shirt. He had not left but there was no doubt in her mind that he was on the point of leaving now.

'Haggard . . . ' She struggled up, groped for him, wanted to grab him and hold him prisoner forever here in this birch grove.

'Don't panic,' he laughed softly, 'I'm not running out on you.'

'I thought . . . ' Sheer relief. Because I thought you were.

'It's almost daybreak,' he dropped into a crouch

beside her, 'and I have things to do today. But I want you in a safe place where I can find you later.'

Her heart was beating fast, maybe she was still dreaming. Or else she had caught him in the act of slipping away and he was making excuses, false promises, to ensure that she did not follow him; he had taken what she had given him willingly, not just her body but her very soul, and now he was casting her aside.

'I want to go with you, Haggard.'

'That's not possible,' a firmness now. 'It's too . . . dangerous.'

'Oh!' Her skin prickled. She didn't care how dangerous it was as long as she had this stranger by her side.

'Listen,' he helped her to her feet, 'this is what we'll do. I want you to go on into the city, follow the main road, don't accept any lifts. When you get there take the road round the clocktower island to the traffic lights, turn left. You'll see an hotel, the King's Head. Book in there.' Something rustled, was pushed into her hand; she recognized the feel of banknotes. 'Stay there until I join you. I don't know how long I'll be, it might be a few hours, even tomorrow, I can't say. But don't leave the hotel. Get it?'

'Yes,' she nodded meekly. She was bewildered but he was the only man in the whole world whose orders she would obey implicitly.

'Tell me something.' There was an urgency about him now, looking up at the sky, seeing how it was grey with the approaching dawn. 'Benjamin, has he any foreign connections? Parents, even close friends?'

She tried to think, the memory of the red-bearded giant who until so recently had been her lover repulsed her. Terrified her. 'I . . . let me think . . . yes, I believe his father was Czech. Or Polish. I can't remember which, he only mentioned it once in passing, never talked about his childhood. I can't say for sure, I wasn't really that interested at the time.'

'It doesn't matter.' Yet judging by the way Haggard gripped her wrist with an intensity that was almost frightening, it most certainly did matter to him. 'It's starting to get light fast now, we haven't much time. Look, there's the road up ahead, start walking along it and duck for cover if you see or hear a vehicle coming. Be on the lookout for anybody on foot until it gets light properly. Now, get going.'

He kissed her quickly and those hours of nocturnal love flooded back briefly. Then he was striding away in the opposite direction, a dark-clad figure almost invisible in the dawn light; hurrying because, as he had said, he had things to do.

She watched until he was swallowed up by the gloom and her spine tingled as an uneasy thought crossed her mind. There had been no pistol hidden in his clothing, she would surely have been aware of its bulkiness as they embraced and kissed, stroked each other. It was gone from his rucksack back at the camp because she had checked. Suddenly she was worried in case he no longer had his gun because she sensed that he might need it and his safety was of paramount importance to her. Without Haggard, life would be nothing now.

Something else, a memory that brought a smile to her lips. For the first time last night she had seen Haggard hatless, his fedora laid carefully on the ground at his side. And now she could not even remember what he looked like bare-headed!

She hurried on until she came to the road, prayed to the God which she had almost forgotten that her man would be all right, that he would be returned to her safely.

* * *

Haggard stood amongst the trees looking across at the hippy encampment in the cold grey light of a summer morning. A sense of dereliction, the occupants might well have abandoned their broken down trucks and buses during the night hours, trekked off to some unknown destination and left in their wake their litter, their ragged washing hung to dry on tree branches, the dead ashes of their campfire blowing in the faint breeze as the nomad urge proved irresistible; just this ruined rusted township as an unsightly reminder of their passage across Cannock Chase.

Except that he knew that they were inside the mobile wrecks, some of them at least, sleeping off their addictions and debauchery, wandering wastrels who despised society and yet fed from it like parasites. Oh, Jesus Almighty, how he had come to hate them after those seemingly endless weeks during which he, in his own way, had been a leech upon their grimed flesh.

Something was bothering him, and right now that was not good. The girl, Penny, he could not get her out of his mind. There had been other women in his life over the years but none of them had affected him as she had. At twilight she had been just a lost shepherdess on a lonely sheeptrack, seeking refuge from the wolves, and he had come when she needed him most. He had never meant it to be anything more than that, even when they had made camp together. If it had not been for the big fellow, Benjamin, Haggard would probably have let her go her own way, for then she had been nothing to him. That moment of weakness had been more than a physical urge, transcended the frustrations of a man whose mission had demanded weeks of celibacy. It was not until afterwards that he realized that he was in love with her. Even then he sought to leave her behind him, he still could. He did not have to go the hotel, she could remain there in safety until the money which he had given her ran out. Now, at this very moment, he told himself that that was how it would be because he had no room in his plans for distractions. He told himself that but he was not convinced.

A movement caught his eye, had him pressing himself back into the dense foliage. A figure emerged from one of the vehicles, a furtiveness about the posture, the way the other checked to ensure that none of his companions were observing him. And even from this distance Haggard had no difficulty in recognizing the powerful form and unkempt beard of the caravan leader who travelled under the name of Benjamin.

Benjamin hurried across the clearing, headed for the gap in the trees, the path that led on down to the wide stream, a shambling gait that was purposeful, a detour that would bring him back to that route which Haggard had taken at twilight. A primordial huntsman in search of prey, tracking his comely mate who had fled from him, deprived him of his most basic needs, his hairy body afire with lust and hatred.

Haggard was not sure, he had to ascertain the other's motives, for throughout those weeks on the same conveyance there had been a barrier between them, one that defied intrusion, concealed dark secrets. Two men whose trails had merged because they had the same destination. First the Gospels, now . . .

The man in black moved with the stealth and ease of a puma. Bent low beneath the overhanging branches he seemed to be scenting the other's trail, stopping every few yards to listen, poised and ready, alert to an ambush. At each bend the path ahead was empty, yet his strained ears detected the brushing of a passing body through overgrown foliage ahead of him.

Haggard heard the traffic on the main road in the distance, recognized that clump of birch trees on his right where . . . he pushed it from his mind, such pleasurable thoughts might mean the difference between life and death, he dared not risk them.

He stared out from the fringe of firs, saw Benjamin ahead of him on an open tract of heather. Once the other turned and looked back, seemed satisfied that he was not being followed. Haggard waited, there was no cover for a stalk, he must focus his gaze on the one whom he pursued, not relax it for a second, determine in which direction Benjamin headed once he reached the road.

The hippy leader hesitated on the grass verge as though unsure himself, as if he had temporarily lost his sense of direction. Then he turned to his right, walked on against the spasmodic flow of early morning traffic, shift workers en route to another day of labouring.

Haggard reprimanded himself for so cursory a reconnaissance, and even that after darkness had fallen. The Gospels, the destruction of their copies, might be his undoing. They were but an incidental, he had placed too much importance on them at the time. He had fallen for the proverbial red herring.

He tensed, wondered if he dared to gamble. Diagonally to his right, half-hidden by the incline, he saw the square of tall pines and beech hedges, enough to tingle his scalp. The Cemetery, it had to be that, and if he took a direct course he could be there ahead of Benjamin, screened from the other's view by the sloping moorland.

Bent double, travelling on all-fours on level ground, the half mile or so seemed to take an eternity. The dew saturated his tight-fitting garments, had them clinging wetly to his lithe body. Then, at last, he reached the fir wood, straightened up, ran until he came to the other side where it bordered a wide, stony track. The empty car park was directly opposite him.

There was no sign of Benjamin. Haggard's fear was that the hippy, in spite of the longer route, had travelled faster along the roadside, had arrived first. He listened, but there was no sound other than songbirds heralding the new day. Benjamin might have gone on past the Cemetery, walked the extra mile or so to the Katyn Memorial. Because if he was not Czech, and happened to be Polish, he was going to pay homage to the 14,000 soldiers of his homeland who had been executed half a century ago. A crime that had been blamed on the Nazis but was later discovered to have been perpetrated by the Russians. But Benjamin was not the kind to pay homage to anybody of any nationality.

Haggard was uneasy, the word he distrusted most was '*if*'; one gambled but never presumed. And then he heard approaching footsteps, ducked back into the trees as he saw the one he was seeking turning off the tarmac road, showering pebbles as he dragged his booted feet down the unsurfaced track.

The hidden watcher was puzzled. Benjamin had spurned the obvious gated entrance to the Commonwealth Cemetery, perhaps out of caution, merely reconnoitring it, a passing walker to any guards who might already have been posted. Access would be easy through the hedge to a determined intruder, Haggard anticipated the other forcing his way inside at any moment.

But Benjamin never once slackened his pace, barely glanced at the hedge, walked on until he was beyond the screened graveyard. Haggard was tense, his scalp was prickling a warning again, accustomed even as he was to the unexpected. Only when the man whom he was following turned sharply left down a grassy track some fifty yards further on and was lost from his view, did the pursuer emerge from his vantage point.

Instinctively, Haggard was aware of wind direction, how it blew from up ahead back towards the last resting place of those servicemen. He heard Benjamin's tread on the springy, dry grass, the cracking of dead fir twigs beneath his feet. The hippy had abandoned caution now, had discarded the possibility of pursuit.

Haggard stood and stared in amazement, for a couple of unwary seconds he would have been vulnerable had not Benjamin had his back towards him, dirt-streaked flesh visible through a jagged tear in the red and black checked shirt. The latter was kneeling on the ground as though he prayed.

Haggard's gaze took in the raised boulder with its metal plaque, read the inscription: THE PEACE VISTA. INTERNATIONAL YEAR OF PEACE. 1986.

It was a kind of secret grotto amidst the pine saplings and bracken, way beyond it acres of scrubland. A hidden place of worship, a shrine of tranquillity set within a hundred yards of the reminder of man's inhumanity to man. The ultimate goal of the itinerant peace convoy who, except for their leader, slumbered in their delapidated vehicles back across the heath.

Benjamin *was* praying, Haggard decided. But not to God, nor to any other deity. The big man struggled to his feet, searched around until he found two lengths of broken branches, one shorter than the other. From the pocket of his soiled jeans he pulled a length of frayed plastic string, began to bind the wood together in the form of a crude crucifix. He worked with an intensity that bordered on panic, a lifetime's obsession that was on the point of being fulfilled. Holding the cross aloft in both hands, muttering incoherently so that spittle frothed on his lips, he drove it downwards, wedged it in the parched ground so that it stood erect and quivering. *Inverted.*

Benjamin was fumbling in his pockets again, had difficulty in extracting the metal aerosol cannister, almost dropped it in his haste. A hissing sound, Haggard saw the jet of purple spray, the way it was played on to the plaque, the childish graffiti scrawl of a football hooligan leaving his mark on the wall of a public lavatory.

Yet, even in its crudeness, there was no mistaking the shape of a pentagon even though its lines were untrue. *A symbol of evil that was epitomized by the superimposed shape of an upturned cross as though the one struck in the ground cast its satanic shadow on to the insignia of its Master.*

Oh, God, Haggard thought, and almost prayed.

Benjamin's huge hands were clasped as though lathering soap, now a harsh rustling sound that was certainly not made by the wind in the foliage. Again, the other was emptying those stuffed pockets; something white and crumpled fell to the ground, began to unfurl, threatened to blow away in the stiffening breeze. Meaty fingers caught it, secured a hold on it.

Sheets of balled newspaper were being heaped with some difficulty and weighted down with handfuls of dry undergrowth, and only when Haggard heard a familiar rattle did he understand, recognized the sound of matches being shaken in their box.

Again he checked the wind direction, knew without any doubt what the other intended, half guessed the motive but that was of no consequence right now. And when Haggard spoke in that familiar clipped voice there was a .38 Smith & Wesson pistol in his hand, the snub barrel trained unwaveringly on Benjamin.

'Just drop the matches, Benjamin. Strike one and I'll blow your head right off!'

Benjamin stiffened but did not turn his head. For a moment he was immobile. Then, slowly, he turned around and Haggard saw that he was still clutching the box of England's Glory, one of the brimstone-headed sticks grasped firmly between the forefinger and thumb of his other hand, held threateningly against the strip of emery paper. The thick lips were stretched in a defiant grin, the hooded eyes blazed hatred.

'Man,' the guttural voice was loaded with malevolence, 'you sure do have a habit of stickin' your neck out. And when I break it, I'm goin' to knock that bleedin' silly hat right off your stupid fuckin' head!'

'So you're going to burn the cemetery, then.' It was a statement, not a question. 'The undergrowth's tinder dry, the wind's right, and once the flames get a hold nothing will stop them. Just a few rows of blackened tombstones left at the end.'

'You've got it. Man, you're fuckin' smart!' Benjamin laughed hysterically; the match made contact with the sandpaper, the finger and thumb were poised in readiness.

'Obviously, you're Polish.'

'Like I just said, you're fuckin' smart. That bastard Jaruzelski had my mother shot. I can't cremate him so I'll do the next best thing and burn the cemetery.'

'That would solve much. In fact, Kosminski might

just like it because it'd be the excuse he and Jaruzelski are looking for to keep the cold war going.'

'Maybe you ain't so fuckin' smart after all, Haggard. It's the Germans I'm after mostly, for what they did to my grandfather in the concentration camps. Their folks can come and look at their blackened headstones and maybe then they'll *realize*! Hellfire came all the way from the Peace Vista to scorch their bones. *And I came all the way from hell to light the fire!*'

'And you're the Antichrist?' Haggard nodded towards the aerosol paint daubs on the stone. Benjamin was mad, of course. Which made him all the more dangerous.

'And now I go to my father.' Suddenly the hippy's eyes glazed, it was as though he was totally oblivious of Haggard's presence. The match scraped but did not burst into flame. It was dragged back, positioned for a second attempt.

'This is your last warning. Drop those matches!'

The film rolled back from Benjamin's eyes, allowed the fury to burn again. 'I guess you're the one who's planning to plant one of those slugs in Kosminski's fat gut,' he laughed.

'Your head's likely to be first if you strike that match, Benjamin!'

'You wouldn't have the guts, man!'

This time the brimstone flared, fizzed and flamed; fell from the open fingers directly on to the pile of newspapers and dried grass. Benjamin threw back his head and a maniacal laugh vibrated from his cavernous mouth.

And that was when Haggard fired. The pistol bucked in his fist, its sharp report deadened by the screen of pines, and Benjamin's forehead seemed to split into two halves.

The man in black moved swiftly, had stamped out the miniature bonfire even as Benjamin's legs buckled. Haggard watched the other crumple on to the scorched newspapers, roll over and lie still, dead eyes turned towards the eastern sky as though anticipating the sunrise, cursing it with his blood-filled mouth.

Haggard was aware that he was sweating, and the hand that held the .38 shook slightly. For one awful moment he had thought that the slug might not have felled Benjamin, that the other was invincible. Which was childishly fanciful, for the Antichrist was an age-old bogeyman, a convenient weapon used by those who preached God. It was called 'fear'. It determined good and devil.

With apparent ease, without even dislodging his fedora, Haggard lifted the heavy corpse, settled it across his slim, powerful shoulders. He bore his burden with practised ease, only slightly bowed by the weight, retraced his steps back towards the road. The early morning commuter traffic had ceased; he crossed swiftly, on down through the pinewoods where, as though drawn by the scent of water like a thirsty beast of the wild, he came upon the deep, stagnant pool.

With scarcely a splash to mark its passing, Benjamin's body opened up a gap in the algae and disappeared into the murky depths.

Only then did Haggard breathe freely, allow himself the luxury of a moment's relief. Antichrist or Pretender, there had been no mistaking the sheer evil which had exuded from Benjamin. If there was an Antichrist destined to return to Earth, then there was no more fitting candidate than the leader of the so-called peace convoy.

CHAPTER FIFTEEN

The only interest which Premier Kosminski showed at the civic reception was in the food. His stoic expression hid his impatience at the delay between courses; a choice of starters, he had opted for both the salmon pâté and the avocado mousse, had devoured them with unseemly relish, his scraping of the bowls audible above the buzz of restrained conversation.

He chewed noisily on the *duck à l'orange*, sucked a wing bone and dribbled grease down his chin, much to the disgust of the mayoress seated opposite him. He resisted the temptation to reach for the cheese board in advance of the pears in calvados. His wine glass was constantly empty, another bottle was produced by an attentive waiter.

Kosminski was drinking more heavily than usual, a fact that had not gone unnoticed by his bodyguards, Andre Orobin and Alexey Kutuzov. They detected an unprecedented nervousness beneath the impassive exterior of the man whose life they were here to protect, at the expense of their own if necessary. The Polish leader was disturbed; if he chose to confide in them the reason, they would listen. If not, then it was not their business to enquire.

Andre Orobin was attached to the Eighth Directorate of the KGB, a man of massive physique, his grey suit straining at its buttons, his neck bulging over the unaccustomed collar and tie. A man of legendary reputation throughout the eastern European countries, his assignments were many and varied. Rumour had it that his brother Georg, the nemesis of *refusniks* prior to *glasnost*, had died after a visit to a secret germ warfare factory. But that was only hearsay that was whispered behind closed doors.

Alexey Kutuzov was smaller in build, his presence was familiar beside Soviet leaders who travelled outside their own country. Insignificant, until you noticed his eyes, tiny pale blue orbs that were sunk in fleshy sockets almost to the point of invisibility, yet they were constantly flickering, fixing those about him with a stare that had them shrinking from him and experiencing a sensation of terror akin to that of a rabbit encountering the hypnotic watchfulness of a bloodlusting stoat.

Both men spoke little, even when they were alone, because there was nothing to say; they were trained in their job, little else mattered. They resented the surrender of their habitual weaponry upon entering British soil, experienced a feeling of defencelessness bordering upon nakedness at being deprived of their automatics. If they complained to each other then they did so within the privacy of their own quarters. They had no confidence in the armed police escorts of western countries.

In the meantime they recognized an uneasiness in their leader, thought that perhaps it was concerned with political strife in their own country and the fear that one day democracy might prevail over communism. The status of premier was not a guarantee of safety even within the current political regime; the penalty for disfavour with the Kremlin was an awesome prospect.

Kosminski took a handful of after-dinner mints, ate them with a hunger that was far from satisfied.

Westerners did not appreciate their food in quantity, it was little more than an excuse for a social gathering. He eyed the leftovers being scraped on to a plate by a waitress, resisted the temptation to devour the scraps in full public view, without shame, which he might have done had they been within his reach.

They had no idea how to make coffee, a watery brew made still weaker with milk. It should be black and strong, drunk with vodka. Port and brandy were bitter to the palate, neither had the strength to fortify a leader. All the same, he drank them. Because he needed spirits to give him courage.

A face, an expression, seen through the bullet-proof glass window of his limousine, was indelibly stamped on his memory. Pallid features, devoid of emotion, yet ruthless in their own way, staring at him out of the crowd, able to penetrate the one-way glass. Seeing him, and hating him. Which was impossible, he had told himself that a thousand times as he had tossed restlessly in his bed last night. A spectre that haunted him, an invincible being that could pass through armed guards as easily as it could see him in his car. Lying there in the darkness, cringing from the shadows that took shape and moved; came close, darted away before he could identify them.

There were voices, too, indiscernible hate-filled, threatening whispers, mocking him because of his terror. Once his thick fingers had groped for the alarm bell but he had snatched them away just as they touched it.

'Is something wrong, Premier?' Orobin would have grunted from the open doorway, his hand resting habitually on an empty holster inside his jacket.

'Yes, Comrade, the darkness, the shadows, they frighten me. Switch on the light and stay with me until daylight.'

Secretly, in years to come, the story would be told and re-told in hushed tones in the workers' apartments. If the premier is afraid of the dark, then we have nothing to fear. It could lead to an uprising of the masses, a revolution. Fear was a weakness which the oppressed capitalized on.

At last the grey light of a summer dawn had infiltrated the bedroom, and only then had Premier Kosminski allowed his heavy eyelids to close. Outside in the corridor his listening bodyguards were relieved to hear him snore. Their leader was not sleeping well, there was something troubling him.

Kosminski did not understand the speeches, made no effort to, because they were the hypocritical recitations of a western idealistic friendship with the Soviet Bloc countries, a thinly veiled attempt to erode communism. Most worrying of all, the ploy was successful, the Wall had already come down. But Poland would resist the tide of democracy until the bitter end, he vowed that.

The speakers were clapped, another rose to his feet as fast as the previous one sat down. Kosminski crunched cracker biscuits noisily throughout.

Now it was his turn. A nervousness, an alien sensation, as he was greeted by a false welcome. He held up his typewritten speech, a slight variation on the one which he had delivered in the NEC conference hall. Lies to combat lies, his guttural tones were translated and passed on by his interpreter.

And throughout the rumbling ovation, Kosminski's eyes roved the packed tables, checked every face within his field of vision, flinched once when his gaze alighted upon a pallid complexion. No, that was not he, the eyes were dulled with boredom like his own, the head was the wrong shape for a fedora.

He was truly thankful that the stranger was not

present. The Polish leader was sweating heavily, his dour features shone in the artificial lighting. An ovation as he sat down, he hated his audience for their falseness, every one of them who had put their hands together. *Glasnost* was a trend; eventually it would go out of fashion, when the cycle was completed, and he was eagerly awaiting that day. In the meantime he must obey Jaruzelski's orders, he had no choice. Secretly he hated the Russians for what they had done to 14,000 of his countrymen half a century ago and had used the Germans as scapegoats. But there was another regime growing, one that was still in its infancy, little more than rumours which the Kremlin dismissed with contempt. In between the workers and the Politburo there was unrest, a resentment by those who were destined to be no more than puppets. It filtered down from the old regime, clinging desperately to Party Secretariat status, to premiers of Soviet countries who would never become leaders, just figureheads who carried out orders, authorized tanks and machine-guns to quell uprisings. Men such as Premier Kosminski who would restore the true power of communism one day, overthrow the Kremlin just as Stalin had brought down the rule of the czars.

It was just a matter of waiting.

Kosminski savoured his gloating but suddenly it had been marred by a stranger's face beneath a ridiculous black hat. Again he tried to tell himself that it was all in his mind, his imagination running riot. He did not succeed in convincing himself.

Another tour of the inner city. He saw the banner before the police moved in and wrested it from the chanting crowds, was not interested in what it said; he was immune to insults, even those which were blazoned in a foreign language. So boring.

Scanning the crowds in the Market Square . . . *searching fearfully for a face* but not finding it.

Then it was back to his country house hotel retreat and the escalating terror which he could not confide to his protectors.

He ate heavily at dinner. Smoked salmon and roast guineafowl in quantity. Wine and vodka in plenty. The place reminded him of the dacha along the Reka Jauza, a tributary of the Moskva, bordered by pine-woods and lush meadowland, where tall pines screened the mansion and wild boar roamed the forests. Once owned by a wealthy Caucasian merchant, Leonid Brezhnev had used it frequently. An establishment where puppet leaders were conditioned.

No luxury was spared. Women were transported there for when the delights of eating and drinking had palled, beautiful whores who gave their bodies willingly to ageing, overweight men. Like himself.

At the dacha the nocturnal hours were pleasurable, there was no time for frightening fancies. But here, on the fringe of a city where God had his temple, there would be no strumpets escorted to his room. The nights were long, the shadows many. Kosminski drank more vodka in the hope that he would sleep soundly.

He didn't.

Orobin and Kutuzov were outside his bedroom door, none could reach him. Armed police were posted in the grounds, dogs roamed the perimeter. None could infiltrate the house.

Except a pallid-featured stranger in dark clothing with the brim of his black fedora pulled low over his forehead in a vain attempt to hide the malevolence in those smouldering eyes.

It was ridiculous! Kosminski thought about leaving the light burning. No. Orobin or Kutuzov would surely notice it and knock on the door to enquire if their leader was unwell. You are not afraid of the dark surely, Premier? He could always pretend to be working. There was no work to be done, his entourage took care of that; speeches were prepared, itineraries checked and re-checked. The only requirement from the Polish premier was his presence.

There was still the threat of an assassination attempt, it had not really worried him until now. You learned to live with that hanging over you. Again, he saw that face on the crowded pavement, now it was lurking in the corner shadows of this luxurious bedroom.

Waiting. For him.

The palpitations in his chest were beginning again, echoing and reverberating in his head, escalated to a roaring noise in his ears. *Like whisperings.*

His eyes peered into the darkness until they hurt. He closed them, lay back on the stacked pillows, tried to will himself to sleep.

Something touched him, softly and icily, on the cheek.

He almost cried out aloud, managed to stifle a cry for his minders to come to his aid. A guttural, strangled gasp slipped from his thick lips, not loud enough to alert those who watched outside in the corridor. He sat up, stared again with aching eyeballs.

There *was* somebody in the room, he discerned a shape in the shadow of the wardrobe, one that merged into a lithe figure, an arrogant, mocking posture, *and it wore a large hat.*

'Who . . . are . . . you?' he asked in a shaking whisper, not loud enough for his guards to hear.

There was no reply. The silhouette had slipped back into the deep darkness, was trying to fool him that it had gone. But it was there, all right.

Hiding. Waiting.

Kosminski was shaking. For the second night in succession his finger trembled its way to the push button of the alarm bell. From there it quivered its way up to the light-pull. But, even at the peak of his terror, the premier was reluctant to flood the bedroom with light which would attract the attention of the guards. And also enable him to look upon that which he feared most.

Are you unwell, Premier? He had to be certain that there was an intruder in his quarters before he raised the alarm. And by then it might be too late.

One quick flash of light; on and off again, his other finger poised over the alarm button. It took all the courage he could muster to tug the cord and blind himself with dazzling artificial light. A second of brightness, then an instant return to kaleidoscopic multi-coloured blackness.

There was nobody in the room. There had been, but they were gone now.

Kosminski chose the lesser of the two evils on offer, the suffocating discomfort of bedclothes pulled up over his head, in preference to the airiness of the huge room with shadows that watched him and touched him with gravelike fingers when he closed his eyes.

Again Chief Superintendent Clive Gardener felt uneasy in the presence of a Metropolitan police officer assigned to special duties. Kids, no more than bloody jumped-up rookies, theory instead of practice and experience, he attempted to assert himself. SAS types, crazy bastards who could use a gun, knew how to kill in unarmed combat. The System used them because there were always situations beyond the capabilities of the average copper. Commandos on civvy street, they gave them a rank and unleashed them. At times such as these.

But they weren't invincible. Tim Walters had proved himself to be the exception to the rule, by whichever yardstick they measured these special agents. They tried to kid you they were real life 007s, Dick Bartons if you were prepared to admit your age. Well, bloody good luck to them! Two killings, a satanic vandalization of the Gospels, maybe by this self-styled crazy Antichrist or a copycat, a peace convoy and a Polish bigwig who was the cause of all the trouble. You're welcome to the lot of 'em, pal!

Detective-Sergeant Mayo; they'd dropped a rank this time, maybe losing too many men. This breed was dispensable. Until you ran out of them.

Another inconsequential, you'd recognize this one by the clothes he was wearing now but give him another suit and you'd lost him. Gardener did not even bother to run his practised eye over the other, there was no point. He was too bloody tired, anyway.

'I've got more men than I can spare already working on the murder enquiries.' Gardener checked a fax sheet from Whitehall, it tied up with the man facing him across the desk. 'Today we have to provide an armed escort for the tour of Cannock Chase, the Commonwealth Cemetery and the Katyn Memorial. Tomorrow's the finale of the Festival in the Close. After that we can heave a sigh of relief and start getting back to normal routine. Like catching Jack the Ripper and this fellow who pretends he's the Antichrist.'

'I'll be around,' Mayo spoke softly, almost inaudibly, 'in my own way.'

'Help yourself, Sergeant, be our guest. If there's anything we can . . . ' The phone buzzed, Gardener lifted the handset and listened. He grunted, carried on listening. The news was bad, in this game they always kicked you when you were down.

Mayo did not speak when Gardener replaced the receiver, did not even ask with his eyes what the trouble was. If the Super chose to tell him, he would do so. If not, then it was none of his business and did not concern him, so it didn't matter a toss.

'That's *all* we need right now!' Clive Gardener prayed that he would not suffer another panic attack; at least, not until he went off duty again. 'Another body! A shooting this time. At Pottal Pool, about half a mile from the cemetery and the Katyn Memorial. Just where we can do without corpses strewn around the countryside!'

Detective-Sergeant Mayo nodded to show that he had heard. It wasn't his place to display emotions. Surprise was an element which you kept to yourself when you were on a special assignment. He stood up, moved towards the door. Murderers weren't his line of business. Only assassinations.

CHAPTER SIXTEEN

Penny was starting to panic by mid-morning. She was convinced by now that this was Haggard's way of getting rid of her, a night of passionate love and now he was dumping her, had given her a hundred quid to make it easier, maybe a sop to his conscience as well. If he had one.

She tried to force herself to hate him, to hate herself for being duped so easily. It was impossible. In her mind she saw his silhouette against the stars in that birch grove, smelled again the male odours which had been so exhilarating. She was in love with him even though he had hurt her deeply. She didn't give a damn who he was, what he was, what he was doing here, the fact that he had been carrying a gun. He was Haggard, the man who wore a black fedora, and that was sufficient.

She had breakfasted well, it was a long time since she had eaten properly cooked food in civilized surroundings. Now she would have to start making plans if he did not show up by tonight. There was no way she could return to the peace convoy, she dared not even had she wanted to. Benjamin would beat her up, maybe kill her. She loathed him, the thought of him ever touching her again was nauseating. He deserved that spotty whore, Diane Wilkes, she was welcome to him!

She thought about returning home, going back to

her parents in Godalming. The idea had material advantages; they would give her lodgings, food, money. But not affection. Rich parents took the easy way out with their children; Penny had spent most of her life up until she was sixteen at boarding schools, and in the holidays she had been sent to stay with friends abroad. You'll simply *love* it at Interlaken, darling, and we've arranged for you to have skiing lessons, too. The Pritchards have a villa in the Bahamas, you'll have a super summer there. We only wish that we could come as well, but Daddy and I have arranged to go on safari in Kenya. You wouldn't like the heat there, the mosquitoes and the poisonous snakes. And next Easter a business friend of Daddy's is taking his family up to a country home he's got in Scotland, a magnificent place right up in the Highlands, and they'd be absolutely delighted for you to go along as a companion for their daughter. I can't remember her name, I'm sure that Daddy did mention it, but you'll have an absolute whale of a time . . .

Going home was a last resort. Penny wasn't going back on the road; she'd had enough of idealism where you kidded yourself you were independent but you were actually living off the state. It had taken two years with that pig, Benjamin, to make her realize that.

And then Haggard walked into the bar, as casually as if he had only been away five minutes, had just popped out to the Gents.

'Hi!' He slid into the seat beside her.

Her hand found his, she wanted to ask, 'Where've you been?' Instead, she said in a faltering voice, 'I was getting worried about you.'

'Listen,' his voice was low, barely audible against the hubbub of mid-morning bar conversation, 'I have to be away for a while, until tomorrow night, maybe the day after. I can't say how long for sure.'

She could not disguise her disappointment. It was no good asking where he was going, what he was doing, because she knew that he would not tell her. But at least he had showed up, and had it been his intention to jilt her then he would not have returned. Would he? There would always be that nagging doubt. She just nodded, had to fight back her tears.

'I want you to stay on here,' bank notes rustled again, 'and don't go far. I'll come for you when . . . as soon as I can. Right?'

'All right.' He was slipping away from her again, her fingers caught his sleeve. 'Haggard?' Oh, God, when whatever it was, was over then he would surely tell her his full name.

'Yes?'

'I'm in love with you, Haggard.' Her thoughts spilled out, she wanted him to know how she felt. And after you've left I might just cry.

He looked at her. It was almost impossible to read the expression in those eyes beneath the brim of his fedora. He seemed lost for words, but when eventually he replied, 'I'm in love with you, too, Pen, but it'll have to wait for now. Hopefully no more than a couple of days,' she could have shouted her delight to the packed bar room.

Then he was gone again, out through the door and into the Festival crowds which thronged the pavements, without so much as a backward glance.

Haggard followed the now familiar route up towards the Close, his pace slowed by the seemingly endless throng of people that were heading in the same direction. The ducks on the Minster Pool were quarrelsome, a couple of large drakes chasing the others away from some soggy sliced bread that floated amidst the scum and litter close to the railings.

The fairground in the park opposite had opened early, its tannoy music harsh and blaring; some men were playing a game of bowls on the adjacent green, white Panama hats protecting their thinning hair and bald heads from the direct rays of the sun. A carnival atmosphere that was building up to its peak; next week the revellers would be gone, their litter swept up and the tranquillity of a cathedral city would return.

Haggard joined the queue which began by the chain-link fencing at the entrance to the Close, two deep right the way up to the cathedral shop. A helmeted policeman walked up and down, hands behind his back, bored because his presence here was a mere formality. It wasn't like a line of soccer fans pushing and shoving in the hope of securing a much-coveted ticket for an FA Cup replay on a first-come, first-served, basis. Here there would be no trouble, neither abuse nor fighting; there were plenty of tickets on sale for the re-enactment of the Cromwellian siege of the cathedral. A thousand £2 tickets, the chief superintendent had imposed a generous limit; you paid your money and on the night you stood where you liked, anywhere on the west and south road where you could obtain a view. The north road was barricaded off, only for VIP spectators and those honoured to occupy the benches on the raised platform which would mostly be filled by the Polish premier and his entourage of interpreters and bodyguards.

The watching constable noted the fellow wearing the large black hat, diverted his attention to the tall chap standing behind in Mexican-style attire, a poncho and even larger headgear, a huge straw sombrero banded in a variety of garish colours. There was no accounting for peoples' taste, he envied them because his helmet was causing rivulets of perspiration to trickle down his forehead and sting his eyes.

But there had been a murder within a few yards of here and for that reason he could not relax his vigilance. He recognized the unmarked Scene-of-Crime car parked up by the school house. Doubtless his plain-clothes colleagues were engaged in a house-to-house enquiry around the Close. Suddenly it did not seem quite so warm.

The double line of ticket purchasers moved slowly. Haggard curbed his impatience, allowed his eyes to rove around his surroundings. There was a regional television unit parked behind the old well, engineers busily unravelling coils of cable; there was no sign of the crew, they were probably enjoying a leisurely liquid lunch, he decided.

A pick-up Land Rover was drawn up alongside the lorry, the tarpaulin removed to reveal two cannons. A couple of workmen in greasy overalls were fastening a winch on to the nearside one. Obviously the time had arrived for the antiquated heavy artillery to be set in place.

The shop was crowded, a middle-aged woman seated at a table in the far corner was tearing tickets out of a book, taking money. Tourists browsed, purchased souvenirs. A lady with a high-pitched penetrating voice was asking about the St Chad's Gospels. She was assured repeatedly that it was only copies that had been damaged and that the originals were now on display in the cathedral. Go through the west door, straight on up to the Chapter House and you'll see them, madam. They are perfectly safe, screened by heavy duty glass, chained and protected, and guarded by a policeman.

Haggard finally bought his ticket and shouldered

his way back through the shop and out into the sunshine.

Armed police with tracker dogs had been scouring the woods and heathland within a half a mile radius of the Military Cemetery and the Katyn Memorial since daylight. A platoon of soldiers from Whittington Barracks joined them soon afterwards, searching bushes and undergrowth, metal-detectors locating hidden empty drink cans; one false alarm yielded a set of lost car keys embedded in the ground. By mid-morning they were satisfied that no assassin had secreted himself in the area during the nocturnal hours, that no explosive device had been planted in readiness.

A military cordon was set up to encompass the acreage which was now declared safe, from now on it was forbidden territory to anybody without an official pass and identification papers. Roadblocks were set up, detours signposted to divert tourists and motorists away from the area. The hippy encampment had been raided again, some drugs and what were deemed to be offensive weapons seized; the eviction order would be served on the occupants after the Festival was over, but right now every available officer was fully employed ensuring the safety of the city's most controversial visitor.

The Polish premier's visit was scheduled for 4.30 p.m. At mid-day the security forces were advised that it had been altered to 3 p.m. Deliberate confusion planned by Whitehall in an effort to disrupt any assassination plot. It might also fool the small minority of protest groups.

It didn't.

Kosminski was tense, the headache, with which he

had awoken after a listless three hour sleep from dawn, had escalated to near-migraine proportions. He had not breakfasted and there was a sour taste on his white-coated tongue.

Today he wore the uniform of a high-ranking military officer; he was deputizing for General Jaruzelski, it would not have been fitting to be viewed by westerners as inferior to a national leader. Only his physical discomfort distracted from his pride, his contempt for the free world.

The demonstrators had been lining the grass verge half a mile from the first checkpoint since 10 a.m: two mounted policemen kept them back but they could not hide them. Because it was a free country.

KOSMINSKI, MASS MURDERER was barely legible, the spray paint had absorbed into the material of the banner, smudged, adulterated the crude lettering. The bearers shrieked abuse, obscenities; the mounted officers drove them back from the road, a girl fell and was lost from view in the bracken. The cavalcade of police motorcyclists and patrol cars passed unhindered, maintained a dignified, almost funereal, pace. The protests had gone virtually unnoticed. At least, Chief Superintendent Clive Gardener, seated in the rear of the dark blue Daimler which followed the premier's Rolls Royce, hoped that it had. He found himself wondering where Mayo was, but that was none of his business.

Kosminski glanced at Orobin and Kutuzov; they looked uncomfortable, probably because they were unarmed. Nobody spoke, they rarely did on such occasions.

The gates of the cemetery were open, the wide steps lined on either side by soldiers in full ceremonial dress, arms presented. The mayor wore his full regalia, seemed to be weighed down by his chain and mace. Senior officers from the three armed services saluted as the convoy drew to a halt.

Kosminski tensed as the car door was opened for him. All eyes were focussed on him, expectancy that became embarrassment when he did not immediately heave his bulky frame up out of the seat. Only his eyes moved, followed a half circle to the extremity of his field of vision; military personnel, police officers, the civilian reception. He scanned them, winced at the pain that throbbed his temples, mentally cringed from each one until finally he had completed his own inspection and there was no merciless, pallid face with burning orbs watching him from beneath the brim of a black fedora.

'It is quite safe,' Orobin muttered.

Kosminski held on to the door as a wave of dizziness came and went. Out into the open, cumbersome and undignified in spite of his uniform, returning the salute shakily. The steps were a mountainside, his feet moved slowly, uncertainly, he was over-breathing.

A deputation closed in on him, an officer carrying the wreath for him as they walked towards the tall memorial. Again, he was checking on his surroundings, starting visibly when a watching grey squirrel bounded from some dense rhododendrons. He consoled himself with the thought that the creature would not have been there had somebody been lurking in the thick foliage.

A graveyard, a place of the dead. He shuddered, licked his dry, thick lips. Just bones; they could not harm you.

He took the wreath, shambled forward, laid it at the base of the monument, straightened up and saluted. On his left were the German tombstones, as white as the skeletons which they concealed. He remembered Katyn forest and how the Russians had blamed the massacre on the Nazis; and *glasnost*, and how cynical it all was.

Kutuzov nudged him respectfully, the deputation wished to move on. A slow, sombre procession, mocked by a chattering magpie from the pine woods beyond the tall hedge. Following the wide grassy track around the New Zealand air force graves; for some inexplicable reason three Germans had been buried alongside them, probably because there was not room to accommodate their remains with the rest of their countrymen.

A single grave, hidden away between the pines and shrubs as though it had been committed deliberately to solitary confinement. Kosminski stopped, felt Orobin bump into him. This lone burial had taken him by surprise, the way an assassin's bullet did. He found himself peering into the shrubs which hemmed them in, this place had a claustrophobic effect on him.

'It is all right, Premier,' Orobin's guttural whisper assured him.

Kosminski stared at the inscription, read it falteringly. 'S.SJT. M.S. WIKTOROWSKI, 13 AUGUST 1948. AGE 48. POLISH RESETTLEMENT CORPS.' He wondered how Wiktorowski had died, why he was here. It was disconcerting, he experienced an urge to flee blindly from this awful place, had to hold himself in check. There was nothing more to see here, surely?

They emerged from the shadows into blinding sunlight, his headache stepped up a gear. Relief because he saw that the entrance gates were still open, an illogical fear that they might have imprisoned him in here. The cars were still parked at the bottom of the steps, an orderly was opening the doors of the Rolls in readiness.

Kosminski fought against vertigo, those steps were

so steep. With relief he fell heavily into the luxuriously upholstered seat of the car, mentally screamed at the soldier to slam the doors shut. Because the bodywork and windows were bulletproof. So he had been told.

Premier Kosminski wished that they did not have to go on to the Katyn Memorial. There was no point, those soldiers had been dead for half a century, nothing could bring them back. He had no wish to have his name added to the inscription on the stone.

Or to be buried in a solitary grave in this hostile place.

Up in the topmost branches of a thirty-foot high Scots pine, immediately opposite the gates of the Commonwealth Cemetery, Haggard stretched to ease his aching muscles. His dark clothing camouflaged him amidst the deep green foliage, rendered him almost invisible from below. Only a creaking of the thick bough upon which he lay full length might have given away his hiding place. Fortunately, it had been strong enough to bear his weight.

Two armed policemen emerged from the undergrowth, hurried to their waiting vehicle. Precariously perched, his fedora part of his cover, Haggard held on to the branch with his left hand, grasped the .38 Smith & Wesson in his right. The butt had imprinted its serrated pattern on his palm, the metalwork was slippery with his sweat.

The security operation had been A1, he grudgingly complimented those responsible for its organization. A thorough search of the area beforehand, a change of timing which he had anticipated, and a bodyguard that hemmed in the Pole throughout so that only a machine-gun could have mown a path through to its intended victim.

Haggard waited. Only when the last police vehicle had moved off did he descend from his perch with an agility which would have rivalled that of the squirrel he had alarmed earlier.

He hit the ground at a run and seized his opportunity to dash across the temporarily deserted road. The cemetery had proved itself to be an impregnable fortress. Even as he moved, fast and stealthily, Haggard was envisaging the layout of the Katyn Memorial, going over every detail again in his mind. And there were also surrounding pine trees which a man could climb undetected, and view from above the gathering in the clearing beyond the small car park.

He wondered if that company of bodyguards would again present such an effective shield for the man they sought to protect from the festering hatred of a fanatical assassin.

The man in black ran with the speed and stamina of a practised athlete. He had timed himself over this route twice within the past week; he estimated that his arrival at his intended destination would be two minutes, fifteen seconds in advance of the motorized cavalcade.

CHAPTER SEVENTEEN

Don Devereux awoke early the following morning, watched the sunrise making latticed patterns on the wall of his hotel bedroom, diamond shapes which he traced with his eyes, found himself counting them. Counting things, anything, was a habit with him when he was preoccupied; eventually it became like a tune that you found yourself humming and couldn't get it out of your head. With an effort he dragged his gaze away, forced himself to lose count. And stopped.

He tried not to recall the previous night, and when that was impossible, he attempted to convince himself that it had not really happened, it had all been a dream. A bad one.

In the end he gave up, groaned aloud at his self-confessed guilt. It had him wanting to pull the bed-clothes up over his head, hide from the world, twist balls of linen in his tightly clenched fists. A deep depression was about to set in, a sick headache was the forerunner every time; it was always the same the morning after he had been with a whore.

In the beginning fear had been the overriding emotion; fear of being stopped by a patrolling police car looking for kerb crawlers in a red-light area. For days he cringed whenever the doorbell chimed, skulked in a back room and pretended that he was not at home, hoped that whoever it was would go away and not return. But in later years he had become hardened to the risks, even thrilled to them. Then a new terror manifested itself, the threat of disease, dying a lingering, wasting death. But even that did not stop him - when the urge was upon him he was powerless to resist its call.

He always paid the price for his obsession on the following morning. He lay there trembling, began counting the shapes on the wall all over again, just in case he had got it wrong the first time.

He blamed Colette because he had to have a scapegoat; she was beautiful, he had first played alongside her in Marseilles, a Victor Hugo dramatization which had run for less than a month. The critics had slaughtered it, damned his career as an actor. He had always considered Quasimodo to be his finest role; they had thought otherwise.

Nevertheless, good (or bad, with hindsight) had come out of it. A whirlwind romance and he had married Colette. For three years they had been happy, scraped a living from the semi-professional stage. But her beauty was his downfall. Pierre Lamont, rising star of stage and screen, had enticed her away with the prospect of the Big Time: Paris, Hollywood, the sky was the limit!

The last time Devereux had seen Lamont's name was on a video film in a hire shop, a low budget saga of the Revolution. That had been three years ago. He did not even know if Colette was still with Pierre. But if only she had stayed with him, the tide of fortune was about to turn.

Don Devereux had abandoned all ambitions of stardom, he had carved out a niche for himself in this era of festivals and centenary celebrations, an entrepreneur who sold a complete package with special attention to local detail. During the winter months he took his bookings, researched the necessary history, engaged his players. His reputation had grown, he was turning work away rather than sub-contract it to amateurs whose clumsy efforts would only serve to damage his reputation.

After the French bicentennial celebrations he was in a position to pick and choose, name his own price. The Lichfield Festival had filled a gap, Ludlow was too small and had been turned down, from next week onward he was fully committed up until the end of October.

He cursed himself for last night, his only consolation was that he had a day in which to recover before the finale. Not a day of idleness, there was still much work to be done, but another full rehearsal was impossible due to cathedral scheduling of other events. He needed to go through the script again; there were one or two small changes that needed to be made. But there was no immediate hurry, an afternoon start would be fine.

If Colette had stayed then she could have shared the glory with him, the rapturous applause of the festival crowds, the speeches and awards, the advance bookings for the following year. Together they could have reaped rich rewards. Now that it was all his, he had no one to share it with. A permanent relationship with another woman, however sophisticated and beautiful she might have been, was out of the question, because it would open up all the old wounds, bleed them; he would compare her with Colette, hate her for not being Colette. Colette had to be punished for her infidelity, for what she had done to him, a thousand times over.

And she had been chastised last night.

A shapely body, features that were hidden in the shadows on the wasteland of a demolition site, but they could so easily have been Colette's. *They were.*

He had degraded her, beaten her because she deserved it, then he had watched her slink off into the night, her sobs sweet music in his ears. She was one of many who had suffered thus, some worse than others. And there would be many, many more, he had to face up to that. A thousand Colettes would pay the penalty for what his very own Colette had done to him!

His anger worsened the pain behind his eyes, lying there in the vengeful solitude of an hotel bedroom was psychological masochism, a festering of his own mind. With a supreme effort he threw the bedsheets back, staggered through to the shower to cleanse himself of the body odours with which Colette had tainted his flesh the previous night.

The past was a spectre, he was truly the accursed. He turned the dial to 'cold', gasped as a deluge of icy water invigorated him. A few minutes later he stepped from beneath it, began to towel himself vigorously. His headache was receding already, those nocturnal hours were evaporating like an autumnal mist in morning sunshine. Only then did Don Devereux come to terms with what he had to do, and, once again, it was the past which was motivating him.

Ron Borg also woke with a headache. He sometimes suffered from 'gun headaches' if he had been shooting for long periods with a weapon which was so light that it recoiled with every shot. The Winchester was certainly no lightweight, so he blamed it on the cartridges; next time he would take his own shells to the shooting ground, spurn their cheap foreign imports which were harsh on the eardrums. He abhorred the use of ear-plugs, an artificial attachment which was alien to the accomplished sportsman.

He swallowed a couple of paracetemols; they would

do the trick. Thank God that there was no rehearsal today, he could not stand another one. That fellow Devereux was getting under his skin. In fact, amateur theatrics were becoming decidedly distasteful to the gunsmith.

In the beginning they had filled a gap in his social life, he might as well have taken up golf except that the game held no appeal for him. Shooting was fine, but it had transcended a pastime; it had become *work*; invitations to driven pheasant shoots, the grouse moors, whatever, were merely an offshoot of his business, a PR job. One needed a hobby which was in no way associated with one's profession, a means of switching off. The amateur stage had appealed, now it was beginning to pall. After tomorrow night, the grand finale, he would finish with it. He promised himself that and felt his headache ease a little.

He had no plans for opening the shop today. There was a backlog of repairs accumulating in his workshop but they could wait. He relished the prospect of a rare day of idleness, a day of no fixed routine, just pleasing himself.

In fact, he would do something which was quite out of character, which, even on a Sunday, he would have dismissed out of hand. He would take the car, go for a drive, a kind of mystery trip with no destination in mind, just see where he ended up.

It was crazy but he would do just that.

Pottal Pool had been cordoned off to keep the ghoulish sightseers back. Clive Gardener despised their sick mentality, that affinity with desert vultures that scented carrion from miles away, drew them to a scene of carnage so that they could gloat over the misfortunes of their fellows, even steal a grisly souvenir if the opportunity presented itself. Road, rail or air disasters, they came in their hundreds, trod the ground like rampaging cattle, obliterated vital evidence.

There had been twenty or thirty of them lining the poolside when he had arrived in the Scene-of-Crime car. They had been ordered back in no uncertain language, a tape barrier erected; they had congregated along the designated barrier, the tape tautened and strained where they pushed forward for a closer look.

A teenage girl had spotted the half-submerged corpse in the brackish water, caught up in a clump of reeds. She had fled up the road, screaming hysterically, stopped a passing motorist. The driver had taken her to Hednesford police station where she was, hopefully, making a statement. The anonymous driver had not stayed, it was always the way. Not that he was likely to be able to provide any useful evidence, it was a waste of time trying to trace him.

A frogman had gone into the water, pulled the body ashore. Later the pool would have to be dragged.

The chief superintendent's chest was tightening up again as though a steel band encircled it. The tips of his fingers tingled. For Christ's sake, don't have another panic attack!

Dead bodies did not worry him, he had seen far too many throughout his career to be either saddened or repulsed. In his mind corpses were *units*, they represented work: investigations and reports. You concentrated on the positive side, that way you retained your sanity. Right now, Gardener was beginning to have doubts about his own.

The fellow had been shot at point-blank range, the pathologist would confirm the policeman's assessment of a single bullet of a calibre large enough to split the skull open, spill out the brains. The features were barely recognizable, just thickset and red-bearded.

The 'death wagon' had been summoned, it should be here any minute. Once the body was removed, the crowds would drift away. In the meantime a CID officer was searching the saturated, algae-bedraggled clothing. He laid the contents of the pockets on the grass, shielded them from the unwanted audience with his body.

Soggy cigarettes, a throw-away lighter. Some vitamin tablets and, in direct contradiction, a phial of what was undoubtedly cannabis. And, finally, one aerosol canister, minus its cap.

'Used to spray obscene slogans on their banners, no doubt,' the sergeant muttered.

'Squirt it!' Gardener thrust his head forward. 'Squirt it on the ground!'

The other looked up, surprise in his expression, his forefinger resting on the nozzle.

'Go on, *squirt it*!' The chief superintendent recognized a hint of hysteria, panic, in his own voice. He might go near-paralytic again; he was contradicting experience, jumping to conclusions. All the same, he had to see the colour of that dye.

'Bright purple!' The officer sprayed a small circle, coloured the parched grass.

Gardener closed his eyes momentarily, and when he spoke again he sounded as tired as he felt. 'The Gospels, the facsimiles, were sprayed with purple paint. Of course, it's a common colour and these dropouts all go for way-out shades. It doesn't necessarily mean anything, we mustn't jump the gun.' I already have.

Where the hell was Mayo? Gardener glanced round, knew he was wasting his time because the Yard man certainly would not be *here*. These chaps were never to be found when your ordinary country copper needed them, they made a point of that. Too bloody high and mighty, chasing top level assassins, and all that crap!

Clive Gardener took a deep breath; okay, there was a long way to go yet, Kosminski's visit to the war cemetery and the Katyn Memorial, but when you had had one panic attack, and were on the verge of a second, optimism was good therapy. The guy who had sprayed satanic symbols on the Gospels was lying right there, *very* dead. If this was the rumoured Anti-christ, then he most certainly was not immortal. He would not trouble anybody again, and there was *just* a chance that he might be the would-be assassin who was stretching police manpower to full capacity. The man they were seeking, travelling as a bloody hippy!

Gardener was trembling, allowing himself the luxury of supposition, trying to believe it, against all the rules.

This fellow could have killed that prostitute, murdered Detective-Inspector Walters. Sure, he could. Guilty until proved innocent, it made you feel a lot easier if you thought of it that way.

Clive Gardener's feeling of relief lasted approximately ten seconds before an awful, nagging thought destroyed it totally. If this guy really had murdered the prostitute and Walters, then there was just one problem.

Somebody had shot *him*.

CHAPTER EIGHTEEN

Haggard moved with the speed of a hunting leopard once he reached the scrubland bordering the Katyn Memorial. Without slowing, crouching, his sneakered feet seemed to sense where every dead twig lay, trod the cushions of grass noiselessly.

He ducked below the view of police and army sentries, gained the sapling pine wood, paused to listen. He heard the hum of approaching vehicles on the adjacent road, the harsher whine of escort motorcycles. So far, so good, he had made it here ahead of them with seconds to spare. But there was no time to linger.

A lofted vantage point was out of the question this time, the trees were too young, did not offer the concealment of the pines by the Commonwealth Cemetery. He stood with his back to a slender trunk, peered through the overhanging foliage. He sucked his lips, watched as the Rolls and its escort drew up on the car park. A door was being held open but the bodyguard and the official welcoming deputation had moved in, formed a protective barrier around the uniformed VIP, obscured the hidden watcher's view. Again, nothing short of a machine-gun or a Kalashnikov rifle could have penetrated them.

'What you doin' here, chap?'

The harsh whisper was like a rapier thrust in Haggard's back; he stiffened, his pulse rate stepped up a couple of notches. He made no move to turn around, just opened the fingers of his outstretched hands to show that he was not carrying a weapon. Behind him he heard the faint rustle of sun-parched grasses, a tread that was as light as his own, knew that the other was now directly behind him.

'I said, what you doin' here?'

'Just walking,' Haggard's reply was instant, still he did not move. 'Hiking. I was out this way, wondered what was going on.'

'Keep right where you are, don't do anything fucking stupid, don't raise your voice. 'Cause we mustn't disturb 'is 'ighness over there, but one peep out o' you and I'll blow your bleedin' 'ead right off! And that won't make too much noise, either, because this little shooter's silenced!'

Haggard studied the soldier carefully as the camouflaged figure moved round in front of him. SAS, no doubt about that, features obliterated by burned cork smears, fifteen stone of solid muscle. The pistol was a .45, the sound moderator giving it an unwieldly appearance, but that was merely an optical deception. In all probability this guy could dent a fivepence coin at thirty paces, hit a running man at fifty. And in close combat he would do a lot of very unpleasant things to his adversary.

'A hippy in a funny hat,' the blackened lips were stretched in a contemptuous leer, 'and a wimp to boot! Jesus, they should build a few gas chambers for you jerks! Now, let's 'ave a proper look at you!'

Haggard's expression was impassive, not even his eyes gave away his feelings; anger with himself at being caught out this way, over-confidence had been his undoing. He had run the gauntlet of a guarded wood, slipped past three or four sentries, but this fellow had spotted him, followed him with a stealth and cunning that equalled his own; bettered it, if he was honest with himself.

'Go ahead and search me, pal. I've got nothing to hide.'

'You don't have no say in the matter.' The pistol was held unwaveringly, trained on Haggard's chest, whilst the free hand ran over his clothing. A human weapon detector, those fingers were sensitive, knew what they were feeling for. A breast pocket was flipped open, the lining pulled out. Squeezing and pinching the skin beneath the garments with masochistic delight. Spinning him round, smoothing down his back, tweaking his firm buttocks viciously as hip pockets were explored. Down the legs as far as the ankles, checking the sneakers.

'Kick your shoes off!'

Haggard obeyed, his socks were rolled down.

'Christ, your fucking feet stink, like the rest of you. You dropouts ever take a bath?'

Haggard did not answer, waited until the other had finished. He was even angrier with himself now.

'Well, you got nothin' on you,' a sigh of disappointment. 'Like I thought, just a hobo parasite livin' off the rest of us. Now, pick up your shoes and *carry* 'em, go right back down that track there and keep goin'. And if I catch you 'angin' about again, Christ you'll be in 'ospital for a month!'

Haggard walked away, did not look back, felt the other's eyes scorching him with contempt now that suspicion had been removed; following him even after the overhanging rhododendron boughs had flipped back to hide him from view, tracking his departure with ears that could detect a fieldmouse scuttling through the grass at twenty yards.

Only when he reached the open scrubland did Haggard stop, pushed his feet back into his worn sneakers. He stood up, adjusted his fedora, smiled whimsically, and realized for the first time that he was bathed in sweat.

That had been a very close call, his damp body chilled just thinking about it.

Premier Kosminski's respite from terror was short-lived; it lasted barely the duration of the short journey from the Commonwealth Cemetery to the Katyn Memorial. Slumped in the luxurious rear seat of the Rolls, he closed his eyes, waited for his breathing to revert to normal. His temples were pounding, he craved a glass of vodka to steady his nerves.

'You are feeling unwell, Premier?' Orobin's whisper was gargantuan.

'No!' A lie that was too emphatic to be the truth. 'It is just the heat.' Meaty fingers waved away further enquiries after his health. I am ill because . . . it is too ludicrous to admit even to himself. The man in black was just a figment of his own mind, a symbolic projection of western hatred towards a Soviet bloc nation that ruled with iron discipline. A chance glimpse of a nameless stranger magnified out of all proportions. Nothing more.

'We are here, Premier.' It was Kutuzov who spoke this time, nasal tones that boomed in the sultry interior of the car.

Kosminski made no move to lift himself out of his seat. It was as though his legs were paralysed, as if he had suffered a minor stroke. Orobin's hand was outstretched, waiting to take his leader's, to pull him upright.

'Thank you.' The premier grasped the proffered fingers, heaved his bulk off the upholstery. Outside he saw a sea of blurred faces, any one of them could have been . . .

. . . the man in the black fedora.

They were crowding him, he was experiencing difficulty in breathing. He wanted to yell at them in guttural anger to give him space. It was so much more claustrophobic here than in the cemetery, a tiny square that had been cut out of the young forest, heady with the overpowering scent of resin and heather. He tottcred slightly, was grateful for Orobin's supporting arm, the wreath which was handed to him seemed to weight him down. Another odour, sweet and sickly, permeated his flared nostrils. *The unmistakable smell of death!*

This place, it might have been the clearing in Katyn Forest, the native pines of his homeland, a huddle of frightened soldiers as they were herded together. He smelled their sour sweat, their fear, heard them sobbing. All fourteen thousand of them.

The memorial stone marked the mass grave, the ground beneath his booted feet seemed to tremble as though some of the interred were scrabbling at the damp soil, trying to dig their way to the surface, had been wounded and buried alive. Muffled cries for help, his ears were ringing with them. The incessant chattering of the machine-guns which had mown them down, echoing through the woods. A magpie, which had been hiding in a bush close by, took off, still chattering and mocking him. A harbinger of death.

The Russians, oh, how he hated them with their hypocritical communistic ideals. Wealth for the bureaucrats, poverty for the masses. Exactly the same as it had been in the days of the czars. Nothing had changed. The Revolution was meaningless, *glasnost* but a veil to deceive the so-called free world. They had sent him here because they feared to come themselves, had sentenced him to be executed on foreign soil so that they might create an international scandal and damn the west in the eyes of their own people. Theory and counter-theory, it was beyond his puppet mind, he knew only that he was the sacrificial victim on a shrine of blood.

Kosminski's eyes were smarting with sweat, blurring the words on his speech notes. It did not matter because his interpreter would translate what he wanted, regardless of anything the premier might say. All they wanted from himself were words, a meaningless jumble.

The premier turned, attempted to see through the crowd, stared in the direction of the woodland on the opposite side of the unsurfaced roadway. It was from there that the sensation of impending doom came strongest, his earlier premonition magnified a thousand times, a waft of summer breeze that was suddenly an icy Arctic wind, heavy with the cloying odour of death and putrefaction. The stench of fourteen thousand decomposing corpses.

The mayor was speaking, reading his prepared speech, a rigmarole of meaningless thanks to a foreign visitor whom they wished had never soiled their holy city with his presence. A mass murderer.

Kosminski only just made it back to his car in time, sinking down into his seat as the wave of faintness came at him, seeing once again in his tortured mind that white face of Death, stark and terrible beneath the black fedora.

Chief Superintendent Clive Gardener wondered if he was going to make it through to the end of the Festival. They now had three unsolved murders and not a single clue. The latest victim was so far only vaguely identified. They had a first name, apparently none of the hippies interrogated had any idea of

Benjamin's surname, nor of his background. They just knew him as Benjamin, they had no idea whence he came before the peace convoy set out on its pilgrimage to Stonehenge. An animal rights activist, he had hinted at vandalizing the Gospels. It all tied in with the Antichrist rumours; the guy even had the paint on him which had been used to spray those black magic symbols on the vellum sheets. A nutcase, and a dangerous one. He had a girlfriend; her name was Penny; again they did not know her second name. She had disappeared a couple of nights ago after a row with Benjamin. Diane Wilkes had vanished, too.

Gardener had descriptions of the two girls, he would circulate their details but it wasn't going to be easy to find them. Theories were all that he had to go on; the desecration of the facsimile Gospels was a far cry from a mutilated prostitute and a murdered special agent. If only Benjamin hadn't got himself shot then, for his own temporary piece of mind, Clive could have pinned it on him. Privately, of course.

Then there was this fellow whom the hippies referred to as Haggard. Gardener listened to the stories of the loner who had travelled with the convoy and who, it appeared, had left for good. The hippies described him. Oh, Christ Alive, what the hell was going on!

Mayo was missing, he had not been seen since that first introductory meeting. He was not replacing Walters as far as an additional guard on Kosminski's hotel was concerned, he had made that clear. He had a roving commission, that was now only too obvious. Kosminski's safety was under the direct control of the Firearms Team. The Commonwealth Cemetery and Katyn Memorial visits had passed without incident; two down and one to go. Just the Big Night left.

All that the chief superintendent could have coped with, then the AC had phoned again. They had had a tip-off from a reliable source that the international assassin, Jean Bourgoin, known by his colourful pseudonym of *The Wolf*, was definitely in Britain. They had probably known for some time and had only just deemed it necessary to pass the information on, Gardener thought.

Bourgoin had landed at Heathrow a couple of days before Kosminski's arrival and the teeming metropolis had swallowed him up. He *might* still be in London. It was doubtful; it would be easier to assassinate the Polish premier in the provinces. Which was why Mayo had been sent to Lichfield, M15 were not prepared to go to security lengths on a par with those that were set up for the Tory Conference in Brighton, one had to get one's priorities into perspective. Far better to set a professional white hunter on the spoor of a man-eating tiger, than to employ a thousand natives to brash out the jungle and attempt to kill the beast with their primitive spears, was how the AC had put it. Which, Clive thought, was not exactly complimentary towards an under-manned, over-worked provincial police force. He admired the chief's confidence in Mayo, but who carried the can if Kosminski got topped?

The assistant commissioner had side-stepped that question.

Madge Gardener resented her husband being telephoned at home, her tone often conveyed her displeasure to the caller. Even to the AC when she had taken his call. And when Sergeant Brooks rang just as her husband had gone upstairs to snatch an unscheduled couple of hours overdue sleep, she asked sharply, 'Can't it wait, Sergeant? Clive has had less sleep this last . . . '

'I'm afraid it's urgent, ma'am.'

Gardener took the call on his bedside extension, he had only just climbed into bed, and his initial fear was that another corpse had been found. God forbid!

'We've found one of the girls, sir!' Personal pride because he was the first one to inform the chief; it was the next best thing to picking up a wanted suspect personally.

Clive Gardener paused, his breathing had suddenly gone shallow, and there was a twinge in his chest as though the muscles were about to tighten again. He recalled that morning beside Stowe Pool, the early sunlight shimmering on the surface, the way the water was slowly turning from pink to claret, the body lapping against the stony shoreline. Oh, God, couldn't you have just have waited until I'd slept an hour or two to find this one? Finally, he asked in a voice which trembled slightly, '*Which* girl, Sergeant?'

As if it damned well mattered. A body was a body unless you knew the person intimately.

'The one called *Penny*, sir. She was booked in at the King's Head, living off the fat of the land. A hippy with a wad of notes in the pocket of her jeans. She's here at the station now, sir. I thought you'd probably like to talk to her yourself.'

'I'll be right down.' Gardener dropped the receiver back on its cradle. He certainly wanted to talk to Penny. More than just that, he wanted to know a lot more about this fellow in the black fedora.

CHAPTER NINETEEN

Operation Werewolf had been set up in 1988, allied to Scotland Yard's anti-terrorist force, a unit comprising highly trained officers under the direct control of Chief Superintendent Wells. It was unique in that it enjoyed an almost freelance role, liaising with Interpol and other Continental police forces, concentrating entirely upon the apprehension of well-known terrorists. It had an advantage over other similar units in that it was not inhibited by boundaries, its officers frequently travelled abroad without restriction, and in less than three years they had built up an impressive tally of arrests, had compiled a hall of infamy surpassed by none, and many of their successes were never made public. Their priority was to save lives, and if, in achieving this, an anarchist disappeared from the scene of international intrigue without trace, then no questions were asked.

Chief Superintendent 'Charlie' Wells operated from M15 Headquarters. In common with the majority of his men he had few distinguishing features. Pass him in Oxford Street or Leicester Square and you did not give him a second glance; you saw a well-dressed clerk on his way to a sandwich lunch or hurrying to the underground. His keen eyesight did not require him to wear glasses but he alternated between a pair of heavy-rimmed and rimless, the lenses of plain glass, perhaps tinted in summer to spare him the glare of the sunlight. He had mastered the art of becoming part of the busy commuter background.

He rarely travelled outside London; he was the spider who wove the web whilst his task force enmeshed the flies. He had little interest in politics, only in those who tried to disrupt them outside the House. He kept abreast of international affairs simply because they attracted fanatics. He neither cared whether the Prime Minister visited Warsaw nor whether General Jaruzelski came to Britain himself or sent an ambassador. Only the implications aroused his interest.

He had no doubt that the plot to assassinate Premier Kosminski was more than a rumour, he would have shed few tears had it succeeded, for those who lived by the proverbial sword deserved to die by it. Wells was sceptical that were the Polish premier to die on British soil it would precipitate an East-West confrontation; nowadays the repercussions of such happenings were trade embargoes and a cessation of diplomatic relationships - both of which had little impact - and in due course the nations concerned resumed a strained return to normality. However, in this instance the Polish visit had attracted the attention of Jean Bourgoin and thus the matter had become a priority. The death of Tim Walters had made it almost a personal issue.

Walters was a good man, too good to lose. Whilst one accepted that officers were expendable, they had to be in a set-up such as this, exceptional men took yeas to replace. You trained officers but experience was a steady progression of self-survival techniques. If you stayed alive then you had proved yourself and you became invaluable to the unit.

Bourgoin had slipped the net at Heathrow. Heads

would roll, he should have been taken at Frankfurt. And there was no better place than London in which to lose your identity, particularly when those who pursued you had only a vague description to recognize you. The Wolf played them at their own game. Successfully.

Wells received the call in his office shortly after midnight. It was terse and to the point; a man had been followed to a house in south London. If the caller had not been Anderson, Wells might just have instructed an agent to keep watch and let the routine wheels roll. But Anderson was of the Walters-calibre, he *never* over-reacted. On two previous occasions he had got his man purely on the strength of his own initiative. But this was too big even for Anderson to handle on his own, and the latter was experienced enough to realize that. Thank God! Had it been Sergeant Mayo then it might have been different.

Wells resisted the temptation to call in the Blue Berets immediately. When a fox went to ground you allowed it time to settle before starting to dig down to it, let its wariness dull in the belief that it was safe. The same applied to wolves. There was no hurry for an hour or two.

He spent some time studying a large wall map, a magnified, detailed street plan of the city. Scholar's Road S.W.12; it would be necessary to cordon off Cavendish and Petney Roads to block The Wolf's rear boltholes, with units stationed on the corners of Sistova and Emmanuel Roads. Rooftop marksmen, it would have to be the Blue Berets, after all; they could not take any chances.

Lichfield and Kosminski had been a self-instigated decoy, their enemy had used their own thinking to his advantage, reinforced it with a false tip-off that the Pole was his target. Get the best men out of town, enjoy the freedom of the city. Walters was already dead. Mayo on a roving commission, temporarily beyond recall. By the time they located him, it might be too late.

Wells did not check on current royalty and cabinet venues, he could do that later if they made a mess of the later Operation Werewolf. For the moment, their man was going nowhere.

Damn it, he needed Mayo in a situation like this. But the fellow would have to be found and he always made sure that he left no spoor. Wells had hesitated over sending him up north, you felt almost vulnerable without Mayo around, but at the time Kosminski had seemed the number one lure for The Wolf.

Sending Mayo *anywhere* ensured that the odd hour's sleep you got was a restless one. He was the equivalent of a semi-trained jungle beast; you were scared to hell to unleash him. He had served with the Gurkhas, the SAS had been just a finishing school after that. Give him an assignment and you knew he'd get his man; your only worry was what he might do to him. At the time it had seemed a foregone conclusion that Bourgoin would turn up in Lichfield and nobody was going to worry too much about what happened to The Wolf. Now the whole thing had backfired, Wells had The Wolf on his own doorstep and he did not have Mayo. Time was at a premium.

Habitually a soft speaker, Chief Superintendent Wells made a succession of phone calls. The AC had to be informed but he would not interfere. A Metropolitan back-up force was necessary in addition to the Blue Berets, the public had to be protected. Evacuate adjoining houses quickly and quietly, have additional marksmen installed before daylight. Once all that was accomplished it might be a long old job, Charlie Wells reflected, and in another couple of days the Lichfield

Festival would be over, Kosminski would have returned to Warsaw and Mayo would be back in London. Which might be handy if the siege was protracted beyond his return; in case, as a last resort, they had to send a man in.

The grey dawn light revealed the barricades, the police vehicles and a couple of ambulances, officers with riot shields, marksmen crouched behind the chimney stacks overlooking the suburban terraced house. It seemed melodramatic, a gross overreaction; in an hour or two the occupant would open his front door and enquire what the hell was going on, why couldn't he take his car past the roadblocks? That pre-siege feeling, Wells was only too familiar with it, it plagued you every time because everything looked so damned ordinary. You told yourself that you had jumped to conclusions, gone over the top. But it could all change in one split second.

You tried to negotiate through loud-hailers, bullets answered you. The man inside did not want food or drink, he had ample cigarettes, an unknown quantity of shells, maybe even a home-made bomb. The unknown factors were the reason why a siege lingered on.

Wells' thoughts strayed back to Mayo again. The fellow would have pleaded to be allowed to go in. If you gave him the go ahead, it was an education watching him. Up on the rooftop, hanging by his fingertips from the guttering, it was anybody's guess how he would have gained entry. But he would have got inside, all right. A single .38 shot and then Mayo would have been opening the door to let them all in. Go upstairs and see for yourselves.

That was the worrying past. Mayo would not be content with simply taking his man out. The Chief recalled a similar situation to this one, a Middle East bomber holed up in a tower block. Mayo had entered by the refuse chute, surprised his man. Oh, God Almighty, you had nightmares about what he had done to that terrorist! Mayo just shrugged, smiled; that was what the Gurkhas used to do to *their* enemies, he had explained. As though that made it all right.

The early shooting was over, Bourgoin had shown his fire-power; one perforated police car and a civilian VW Golf with its windows shattered and its tyres flat. Later, maybe tomorrow, even the day after, he would finally accept that nobody was conceding anything. In the end he would be the loser; Wells had to ensure that The Wolf lost all on his own, that he did not take anybody with him.

It was going to be a long sit-in, the kind where you did a lot of soul searching. Wells thought again about Walters, wondered who it was who had managed to take him by surprise, stick a knife in his back. If it was not Bourgoin, and it clearly was not now, then it was somebody of The Wolf's calibre.

Which meant that Premier Kosminski might be assassinated after all.

The girl who called herself Penny was pretty, Gardener grudgingly admitted. She came from a good background, middle-class parents who gave their offspring everything except that which mattered most. Indirectly it was all their fault; but that was none of his business.

She was visibly shocked when he informed her that Benjamin had been murdered, but she confessed readily that she no longer had any feelings for the fellow.

'I just tagged along with him,' she lowered her eyes and her interrogator detected shame where there might have been sorrow. 'But when he hit me, that was it, I'd had enough. So I left. That's all there is to tell, I haven't set eyes on him since.'

'You had a companion on your flight.' A statement, not a question.

'Haggard?'

Penny's lips tightened, she made no denial of it but Chief Superintendent Gardener recognized an all too familiar stubbornness. She was not going to go out of her way to tell him about her latest lover and he was too damned tired to make her. It would all come out eventually. She had committed no crime, he was only entitled to question her, not interrogate her.

'I need to find this man Haggard,' he spoke wearily, almost kindly. Just tell me about him, make it easy for me. 'He gave you money to stay in the hotel, didn't he?'

This time she remained silent.

'I must ask you to remain here for further questioning,' he said. 'There has been a murder. We have to find out who killed Benjamin, catch the killer.' He glanced at the sergeant standing in the doorway of the interview room. 'I'm going to leave you now but I shall be back later. Think it over, my dear. You might be able to help us and by doing so make life a lot easier for yourself.'

Suddenly the man in the black fedora was more important to Gardener than anybody else.

Madge was watching the television when Clive Gardener arrived home. An extended news bulletin, a siege somewhere in South London.

'That's the last thing you want to watch.' She switched the set off as he entered the room, mutely defied him to turn it back on.

Miraculously, his tiredness had left him, somehow he had gone through the fatigue barrier, felt temporarily refreshed, but it would catch up with him again. Roll on tomorrow night then I can get some real sleep.

The moment the phone rang he knew that it was the AC calling. A premonition. He beat Madge to it by an outstretched hand.

'There'll be a news flash shortly,' the AC sounded weary, too. 'But there's something you have to know. The Balham siege . . .'

'It's just been on the box.' My wife thinks I ought not to watch it; *Neighbours* would be better for me.

'Recorded pictures. It ended a few minutes ago. The guy panicked, came out shooting. He was shot dead.'

'Oh!' Not that I'm really interested.

'We're virtually certain that he's Jean Bourgoin, The Wolf!'

'Oh!' again. If they've shot him then that means he's not in Lichfield, that he's not here to assassinate the Pole. A feeling of relief, almost euphoria. It was shattered instantly.

'We've got The Wolf,' the other said, 'so that means that we haven't got a clue who is operating in your area. But whoever he is, he's no amateur. I want you to get hold of Mayo as soon as possible, it's vital that he knows the latest turn of events if he doesn't know already. We are up against a dangerous enemy, a fanatic, and believe me, Chief Superintendent, only Mayo is capable of handling this now. Find him, there's not a moment to be lost!'

Clive Gardener groaned inwardly as he replaced the handset, felt his chest beginning to twinge again. He sensed his wife's disapproving stare, kept his gaze averted.

'I have to go out again, dear,' he sighed.

They were making too much of this Mayo. Christ,

he was only a bloody *sergeant*! By the way the AC had talked you'd think they had lost contact with the commissioner himself. If Mayo was all they cracked him up to be, then how was it he was still in the lower ranks? It inflated the bloke's ego, made him arrogant. Right now he was probably sitting in one of the pubs drinking a pint. All the same, Gardener had his orders to try to locate the other.

And that was not going to be easy.

CHAPTER TWENTY

Don Devereux's depression had subsided along with his headache. It was as though the night had been an obstacle to be surmounted, an unsavoury task that had to be done and now it was behind him. It would happen again, of course, but he would meet it when it arose. In the meantime, there was work to be done and now an obsession of a different kind was driving him on.

Lichfield Festival was different, this time he was not performing to an audience of anonymities, his talent was on show for the benefit of the puppet dictators of Poland. His lips tightened at the thought, he hated the regime for what it represented - oppression and bloodshed! And tonight when he took his final bow it would be before a mass murderer, a fiend with all the traits of Hitler's generals. Devereux could not forget what the Nazis had done to France, to Paris. But the thought must not detract from his performance because he was a professional. The Big Night, the finale, must be one that would never be forgotten. By those who watched as well as himself.

His actors were already beginning to assemble in their separate venues. Fifty or more Parliamentarians in full costume were even now gathering on the Cathedral School playing field, the Warwick and Coventry garrisons merging to launch an onslaught on the Close, awaiting the arrival of Lord Grenville Brooke who would ride at their head.

The Royalists were preparing to defend the Close, the crowd barriers ideally suited as barricades against the armies of Cromwell. They must be ready long before darkness fell, the audience thrilling to the atmosphere of the pending siege, their sympathies divided - for there were those amongst them who would delight in the overthrow of royalty. Devereux promised himself that his carefully prepared realism would whip their emotions into a frenzy. They would step back three centuries in time, they would become part of the ensuing battle.

His hand trembled as he checked the leading cast in the impressive full-colour programme:

Lord Grenville Brooke	Don Devereux
Sir John Gell	Ronald Borg
The Earl of Chesterfield	Nigel Jameson
Dumb Dyott	Philip Page

Their photographs, in full regalia, were on the frontispiece, taken at the first dress rehearsal. There was a brief synopsis of the three sieges on the following pages; which was a pity, it was akin to reading the plot of a book in the blurb on the back cover, an insult to reader intelligence by the publisher, a presumptuous arrogance that the text might not be fully comprehended.

Perhaps history would be rewritten tonight, he smiled to himself at the thought. The future was always unpredictable . . .

Ron Borg was busy loading the muskets, explaining to those whose role it was to use them how they were charged and fired. Sachets of black gunpowder, three drams per loading, a piece of wadding rammed down to hold the charge in place. A report, a cloud of villainous smoke; there was no danger. Yet the police had checked again, they were taking no chances.

Borg stood back watching the inspecting officers with contempt as they examined the flintlocks; the recent Firearms Amendment Bill had backfired on the law, overloaded it with work and placed unnecessary restrictions on law-abiding gun owners, the very section of the public who would take the most care to ensure that their firearms did not fall into criminal hands. Outlawed weapons such as repeating shotguns had been sold cheaply, prior to the new legislation, the black market was flooded with unwanted guns, the criminal element had seized upon an unprecedented opportunity to arm themselves. The full price of this latest piece of folly had yet to be paid.

'We'd like to have a look at the cannons, sir,' that same officer, officious in his icy politeness, already making his way to where the pair of big guns were mounted on the south side of the Close in readiness for the coming of Cromwell's soldiers.

Borg tensed, he waved a hand in the direction of the heavy artillery. There you are, go and look for your bloody selves! He watched them closely but offered no assistance.

The two uniformed policemen walked around the cannons with an air of nervousness, as though the guns might suddenly detonate their objection to this intrusion upon their centuries-old secrets. One of the officers shone a torch down the nine-inch barrel, peered inside.

'It's loaded, sir!' An accusation, an almost gleeful tightening of the facial muscles.

'It is, officer. Just powder and wadding. In accordance with the regulations laid down by the church and the police for the siege.'

The policeman turned away, his gaze alighted on an array of cannonballs piled at the foot of the mounting, his expression one of distrust and suspicion in his diligent search for some irregularity, some breach of the Firearms Act. 'Those are *cannonballs*, sir!' You stated that the cannons were only to fire blank charges. You lied! Accusing, secretly gloating, unbuttoning a tunic pocket as though he was about to record the illegalities.

'They're polystyrene,' Borg replied. 'Pick one up, see for yourself, officer.'

The constable flushed. Perplexed and angry, he looked to his companion for support but the other appeared not to have heard. He stooped, lifted up one of the steel grey objects, examined it; it was slightly larger than a tennis ball and virtually weightless.

'See what I mean, officer?'

The policeman tossed the ball back on to the pile; it bounced, rolled away as a waft of summer breeze caught it.

'Actually, they represent *grenados*, officer.'

The other stiffened, scowled. He did not understand but he was not going to make even more of a fool of himself by asking what a grenado was.

'Cannonballs filled with gunpowder,' Borg's tone was condescending as he pushed home his advantage. 'There's a reference to them on page four of the programme, if you're really interested. The seventeenth century equivalent of mortars, that's what the main structure of the cathedral was demolished with. I was taught about them at school.'

The policeman walked away; Ron Borg knew that they would not check the weaponry again.

The crowds had begun to file into the Close, channelled through the checkpoints where cathedral guides, supported by uniformed police officers, scrutinized tickets. A carnival atmosphere, a multitude of gaudy costumes, shouting and laughter. Alcohol was forbidden within the precincts of the cathedral, already a dozen or so cans of lager had been confiscated by the police. They frowned at Coke cans, grudgingly allowed them to pass unhindered; an army of council roadsweepers was scheduled to begin clearing up the inevitable litter at six o'clock the following morning. There was always an unsavoury side to every showpiece on this scale, but the cathedral restoration fund might achieve its annual target as a result of tonight and that was all that mattered.

Haggard showed his tickets, moved on. A policeman watched him go, noted that he had opted for a south-facing position, almost immediately opposite the VIP stand. A weirdo, maybe he supported anarchy, was psychologically backing the Parliamentarians to overthrow the besieged Royalists, had chosen to join Cromwell's troops behind the cannons. It was just an idle speculation.

Haggard had spent a busy, if seemingly futile, day. He had resisted the temptation to return to the hotel and check on Penny. With an effort he had pushed her to the back of his mind, for she would have been a distraction, albeit a pleasant one, to his alertness, his wariness. He was tense, his ability to relax his mind and body had temporarily deserted him.

His thoughts went back to the Peace Vista, he saw again that evil bearded face explode like an over-ripe tomato hurled at a wall, obliterated by the bullet from his .38; the way the corpse had floated obscenely in the murky pool before becoming caught up in a reed bed and submerging slowly.

He had shot Benjamin on impulse, he had not needed to kill him. A broken leg would have sufficed, he had had no cause to use his pistol other than as a club, he could have overcome his adversary without it and still put out the blaze.

Haggard gave up trying to tell himself that it was not for Penny that he had killed. Because at that moment he just knew the big fellow as Benjamin, a crazy hippy. Had he known what he knew now, then it would have been easier because he could have convinced himself that he had killed for a different reason.

Ultimately, though, it made no difference. And he had a strong premonition that he would kill again before this night of pseudo-carnage was over.

Kosminski was started out of a listless doze by a heavy knocking on the door of his hotel bedroom. From out on the landing he heard Orobin's husky whisper.

'It is almost time to go, President.'

'All right!' Annoyance, he experienced difficulty in speaking aloud, his mouth was dry and that same sour taste lingered on his palate, the flavour of pine trees and heather, laced with the taste of putrefaction that had seeped up through the soil from that mass grave. The floor seemed to quiver, as if in a grotesque reminder of bodies that were buried alive and dug desperately with their fingers in an attempt to claw their way up to the surface.

Early evening sunlight bathed the half-timbered room in a golden hue; for a few moments the premier was totally disorientated, was convinced that it was morning and he had awakened from yet another troubled night. But the nocturnal hours were still to come.

His uneasiness was merging into terror. He remembered the cemetery, and how it had been at the memorial where Death's icy fingers had stretched out and touched him. He grunted, swung himself out of bed, crossed to the window and looked down upon sunlit grounds, shrubberies in full bloom. So peaceful and yet . . . A movement in the foliage attracted his attention. He shied from the shadowy outline of a man standing amidst the rhododendrons, a figure that stood and watched the house, had a gun resting in the crook of his arm. Instant relief because he recognized the other as an armed policeman; it should not have concerned him because in his own country he never travelled without a full military escort. Here, in Britain, death still stalked him; *Death in the form of a black-clad figure with a pallid face and smouldering, malevolent eyes. The personification of evil lurking in every dark place.*

You are stupid, he tried to tell himself. Orobin knocked the door again, more urgently this time.

'There is not much time left, Premier.'

Not much time left. The words were chilling, uttered by those cruel lips beneath the black fedora, barely audible against the jeering of a crowd of protestors.

In that instant Kosminski determined that he was not going to attend the finale of the Festival. He would remain here in this room, leave the light burning all night, not close his eyes until his plane took off from British soil on the morrow.

'Orobin . . . *I am not going tonight!*'

The bodyguard stared in disbelief, opened his mouth to protest, closed it again. It was not his place to question the Polish premier, and yet . . . he had been entrusted with the responsibility of ensuring that this visit went according to schedule, his task was not solely to protect his leader. General Jaruzelski had appointed him for the British visit with those explicit instructions. It was almost as if the general had no faith in his deputy. Or maybe did not even trust him.

Orobin swallowed, clenched his huge fists in frustration.

'I am not well, Orobin.'

Orobin scrutinized the other with frightened eyes. That was certainly true: he saw ashen features, the eyes puffed and staring as though with a fever, the hands shaking uncontrollably as they were wrung together. Orobin sighed; when one was ill, one was ill, and there was nothing that anybody could do about it. Even General Jaruzelski had once cancelled an engagement because of influenza. He said, 'I think you should see a doctor, Premier.'

'When we return to Poland. I have no wish to be examined by a physician here. Once they confine you to bed there is no knowing when you will get up from it. No, I shall rest here until tomorrow morning, sleep on the plane as well. And if I feel no better when we arrive in Warsaw, I shall ask a doctor to see me.'

'But the Festival, Premier . . . it is the climax to your visit, the city is seething with people who wish to catch a glimpse of you. You will be seated throughout, there are no speeches to be delivered. The evening is warm, you will come to no harm. Just two or three hours and then you can relax, it will all be over.'

It will all be over.

Again Kosminski recalled that face that had peered into his car, seen where it was impossible for other mortals to see. You could tell that the stranger had seen, had singled out his prey, a nemesis who was invincible to armed guards, to whom strict security arrangements were no more than an encumbrance which was easily thwarted. The devil in human form.

'I . . . I don't think that it would be wise for me to go tonight, Orobin.' Kosminski moved back to the window, looked out. The shadows on the lawn were already beginning to lengthen. There was no sign of the armed guard, he was probably asleep in the shrubbery. Still watching and waiting. But his presence, his weapon, would be futile against . . .

Orobin experienced a rare twinge of panic. If Kosminski cancelled his engagement then the general would be furious. It was obvious that the premier was terrified, had been so since his arrival in this city. Jaruzelski was frightened, too, the bodyguard would not have dared to whisper it even to his closest ally, Kutuzov. But he knew only too well that Jaruzelski had sent an ambassador because he was afraid to come himself; because of Gdansk and a lot more besides. He dared not face the British public, the Poles who resided here. If there was to be an assassination then the victim would be Kosminski. Perhaps he, too, sought an international incident, one that would distract the eyes of the world from the growing unrest amongs the workers, the rumbling tide of democracy that threatened to swamp the communist regime which was beginning to lose its iron grip on the country. One never understood the communist mode of thinking, not even when one was a tiny cog in its mighty engine. The Kremlin was treacherous even in the midst of *glasnost*.

'Premier . . . '

'I am *not* going, Orobin!' A hoarse croak that was almost a shout. 'I have told you once, I will tell you again . . . '

'Premier,' Orobin held up his hands, 'let us not panic. I think that you must be seen by the public tonight, and I see a way to compromise, one that will not anger the general nor inconvenience yourself.'

Kosminski listened, did not interrupt, and when Orobin had finished speaking, he nodded his agreement to his bodyguard's suggestion.

* * *

Haggard had an unrestricted view of the Polish guests of honour, or rather, of the stately Rolls Royce as it was escorted into the Close, the floodlights glinting on its silver grey paintwork, the passengers hidden behind dark glass. The cavalcade wove its way up the north road, disappeared through the entrance to the old bishop's palace. Now there were police everywhere, the officers who had been on crowd control trebly reinforced; the atmosphere had taken on a sombreness, you had the feeling that the cathedral might really be under siege, that you were trapped inside its defences, at the mercy of the attackers.

The VIPs' dais was bathed in shadow, Haggard saw how the platform had been sited on the edge of the sloping, upper lawns so that none of the lights shone or reflected on to it. A shrewd move to ensure that the Polish premier was no easy target for a marksman hidden in the crowd.

The deputation walked to their viewpoint from the palace, again their route was shadowed by the giant leafy chestnuts, a line of stiffly moving silhouettes climbing up the wooden steps and vanishing into the obscurity of their seats.

Somebody further along from Haggard yelled abuse, a string of obscenities directed at communist oppression; two policemen moved quickly into the crowd and a struggling youth was dragged away to a waiting Black Maria. The line of elevated statues up on the cathedral, kings of stone who had overlooked celebrity occasions for centuries, seemed to scowl their disapproval. The audience found themselves talking in whispers, suddenly overawed.

Royalist actors emerged unobtrusively from the west doors of the cathedral, took up their positions. One, a tall stooping figure, carried a musket of extraordinary length, seemed top heavy when he shouldered it.

'That there's Dumb Dyott,' a middle-aged woman behind Haggard whispered to her husband, 'Lord, I hope that gun isn't really loaded, somebody might get killed if it is.'

Somebody might get killed.

The man in the black fedora was tense now, his eyes never still. He stared into the background shadows directly opposite, and after a time he thought that he could recognize the outline of Premier Kosminski in the front row, armed guards above and below him.

Suddenly the sky to the east was ablaze, fiery rockets that arced, exploded loudly in showers of sparks, reports that were magnified across the expanse of Stowe Pool. The fireworks display had commenced, the signal for the gathered Parliamentary armies to begin their march upon the cathedral.

CHAPTER TWENTY-ONE

The city of Lichfield had been of paramount military importance to both Royalist and Parliamentary forces during the Civil War. The former had established their headquarters in Oxford, the latter in London, and both factions needed ports and communications for importing armaments from the Continent. The north of England was loyal to the king, the south to Cromwell.

The main route to Oxford passed through Lichfield, close to the cathedral, and many convoys of arms travelled this way unhindered. If Lichfield fell to the Parliamentarians then this supply would be cut off and Cromwell would be virtually assured of victory.

Lord Grenville Brooke had arrived in Lichfield, an awesome sight astride his black stallion, his plush cassock ruffling in the breeze, his cruel features hidden behind the visor of his helmet. A fanatical Parliamentarian, his very presence instilled fear amongst the ranks of soldiers who lined the field adjacent to Stowe Pool. A huge bonfire, a welcoming beacon, cast a scintillating glow on steel helmets, exploding fireworks filled the night air with villainous smoke, a forerunner of the battle to follow. The crowds cheered this invincible giant for whom victory was assured.

The Warwick and Coventry garrisons had marched

throughout the day to join him here, followed soon after by the Earl of Essex's army, a mighty combined force bent upon the destruction of the cathedral and the overthrow of the king.

'Long live Cromwell! Destroy the cathedral!'

Brooke wheeled his horse, motioned to the soldiers to follow him. He stood erect in the stirrups, surveyed the night sky with its myriad of stars. Rockets criss-crossed, exploded, but he ignored them. His followers came to a halt behind him, every one of them scanning the heavens. Looking for a sign from God before they entered into battle.

But there was none, just fireworks and stars.

Onward, a heavy tramping of booted feet, kicking up dust on the narrow footroad until they reached Dam Street, the silhouette of the cathedral rising up before them as though defying them now as it had its enemies centuries before.

Grenville Brooke dismounted, he was clearly ill at ease. He knelt briefly, prayed unashamedly. The watchers fell silent, they sensed their leader's foreboding and were afraid.

Lord Brooke rose, climbed back into his saddle. God had not given him a sign, he would rely upon his prayers being answered; the armies were ready, it was too late to turn back now. Ahead of him he heard the crack of a musket, the defence of the Close had begun.

He urged his mount forward, it threatened to shy as the boom of a cannon reverberated throughout the Close. He smelled the acrid stench of black gunpowder in the air, wrinkled his nostrils. Sir John Gell had arrived, ridden non-stop from Derby, had already started to shell the defenders. There was no time to be lost, his greatest fear was that the Royalists might surrender to Gell in the face of heavy fire, that there would be no commendation from Cromwell for his own endeavours.

Gell's soldiers lined the south road, crouched behind the low stone wall, musketfire was spasmodic. Brooke bent low in the saddle, looked for the man he sought, spied him by the furthermost cannon, loading a charge of powder into the huge barrel, seemingly oblivious of the danger from the besieged. More shots but the small man continued with his task, did not look up.

'Sir John Gell!' Brooke was forced to shout to make himself heard above the noise of battle. 'Welcome to Lichfield in the name of Cromwell!'

'My lord,' the other glanced up, looked somewhat ridiculous in his protective helmet with the rimless glasses behind the visor, peering owlishly through the smoke. 'Your arrival is timely, we have driven them back into the cathedral but a few *grenados* will soon make short work of the masonry.'

Brooke dismounted, there was no mistaking his arrogance. His arrival was timely, indeed. Another half hour and it might have been all over, this small force from Derby having achieved that which the combined armies of the Earl of Essex, the Warwick and the Coventry had been sent to accomplish.

'There will be much fighting yet,' Lord Brooke boomed.

'We shall see, my lord.' Gell waved his gunner to one side, appeared to be delving into the pile of cannonballs, causing them to roll and betray their weightlessness, as if searching for something. 'Ah!' He weighed a ball in his hand. 'A grenado, the enemy will scuttle from their frail cover. Have your men ready to take them as they flee like rats from a burning building!'

'Who is that fellow?' Brooke turned, pointed to

where a tall bony figure stood amidst the billowing smoke, gaunt-featured, clothed in peasant rags, a huge fowling piece mounted threateningly to his shoulder. One who defied not only Oliver Cromwell's soldiers but death itself. Surely, any second, the soldiers would cut him down.

That is Dumb Dyott, my lord,' Gell answered scathingly, 'a local folk hero, I believe. He is mad, if he were not then he would be trembling in the cathedral with the rest of them, foolishly believing that stonework is invincible to the might of Parliament.'

'Dumb Dyott . . . ' Grenville Brooke stared, lifted his visor to enable him to see more clearly. 'A scarecrow of a fellow, damn his impudence!' His gaze shifted to the soldiers on his right. 'Cut that man down!'

A shot rang out, a thunderous report, sparks and smoke belching from the muzzle of the long gun, that scrawny apparition reeling from the recoil, staggering back.

For a second it appeared that the ball had missed, had arced over the buildings at the rear, maybe its trajectory taking it as far as the Minster Pool. Then, slowly, the bulky form of Lord Grenville Brooke crumpled to the ground, rolled over and lay still, arms outstretched.

A gasp went up from the onlookers, a cry of disbelief from the foot soldiers. '*Dumb Dyott has shot Lord Grenville Brooke*! It is a bad omen, he should have heeded God's warning when there was no sign given!'

Sir John Gell was on his knees, hastily examining the fallen man, looking up with horror. 'Dumb Dyott has shot him in the eye, a feat of unbelievable marksmanship!'

All eyes were turned back to the Close, the ragbag of a musketman holding his weapon aloft, his wild victory cry chilling the blood of all who heard it.

'It is a sign,' a soldier muttered, 'we must withdraw, God is on the side of the king!'

'Fool!' Sir John Gell turned angrily on the clustered soldiers, saw how they shrank from him. 'It was a lucky shot, it might have killed any of us, or none of us. Lord Brooke is dead, and *I* am instructed to take command in the event of such a happening. *Now watch, see how the House of God will stand up to an onslaught of grenados!*'

Haggard had pushed his way along the front of the audience, ignored the muttered protests from those spectators whose view he obscured. His eyes, his concentration, had been focussed solely on the big man who now lay motionless in the road. You could almost believe that he was really dead; except that it was a re-enactment of history, in the actor's script, and it could not have turned out otherwise. Brooke had been shot by Dumb Dyott three centuries ago; he had to be shot again now. All the same, he found himself wishing that it was reality, for had Don Devereux been dead right now, the danger which the man in black was anticipating would have ceased to exist. He was tense, wary of a trick. Surely it was some kind of ruse. His hand tilted his fedora back on his head, his slim fingers eased up inside it.

The cannon and musket smoke had eddied towards the watchers, Haggard coughed as it seared his lungs, the saltpetre stinging his eyes and blurring his vision. Once again he visualized the red-bearded hippy leader, recalled the other's words as he prepared to ignite the undergrowth and send an unstoppable wall of flames towards the Katyn Memorial. 'And now I go to my father'. At the time Haggard had assumed that it was a reference to Benjamin's supposedly satanic master.

But now he guessed, *knew*, otherwise. Oh, Jesus

Christ, it might be too late already! This was the moment for which he had travelled hundreds of miles, spent weeks of watching and waiting. The attempt had not been made at either the Commonwealth Cemetery or the Katyn Memorial. So it had to be here, *because this was the final throw, the assassin's last chance, and after tonight it would be gone forever.*

He elbowed away somebody who was crowding in on him, and with his other hand he surreptitiously slid the .38 Smith & Wesson out of its reinforced holster inside the sweatband of his fedora; pulled it out, held it so that it was screened from the view of those around him. His smarting eyes were still focussed on that crumpled body on the tarmac, again he was almost convinced that Don Devereux was dead. And that would have solved a lot of problems.

In the distance, maybe seventy-five metres away, obliterated by the swirling powdersmoke, stood that raised platform with its Polish guests of honour. To Haggard's left Sir John Gell had completed the loading of the cannon with its supposedly hellish gunpowder-filled cannonball. The packed crowd had entered into the spirit of the siege, were shouting to warn the Royalists who sheltered in the cathedral. There was no sign of Dumb Dyott; he had either been shot or had fled back inside to join his companions.

'Sir John,' a captain stepped forward, 'a messenger has arrived with the tidings that Royalist reinforcements are on the march from Tamworth and Rushall to attack us in the rear.'

'Then we shall see how they fare against this heavy mortar!' There was fanaticism in Gell's tone as he turned back to his cannon. 'Damn them. And damn all Royalists!'

Haggard stiffened, anticipated that Devereux would stir, suddenly spring to his feet, had the barrel of his gun trained upon him. Surely the other would make his move at any second, he *had* to. But the man playing the part of Lord Grenville Brooke to perfection continued to feign death.

Haggard's stomach knotted. Somewhere at the climax it had all gone dreadfully wrong. For himself, too.

The huge mortar gushed fire and smoke, an iron dragon roaring its wrath so that the ground around it trembled; a flash which blinded the watchers temporarily, deafened them, had them turning away, holding on to one another. Haggard averted his gaze temporarily in an attempt to regain his vision, glimpsed Devereux still lying on the ground, not moving. God, he must have been wrong.

He knew that he wasn't.

Almost simultaneous with the thunderous report of the cannon came a devastating explosion up on the north road. *A fireball that leapt for the night sky, shrivelled the overhead horse chestnut foliage in one mighty tongue of flame, destroyed the shadows instantly. Blinded, yet the watchers saw it and began to scream hysterically. One split second glimpse was enough; stout woodwork was reduced to flying, burning kindling, fire-blackened bodies tossed into the air as though hellfire had erupted beneath their vantage point, their clothing blazing and the smoky air filled with the stench of roasting human flesh.*

Surely, this was the coming of the Antichrist in all his hellish glory!

Scattered smouldering lifesize rag dolls lay amidst the wreckage, their edifice blown asunder with the force of a Semtex bomb, the entire Polish delegation annihilated even before the echoes of that cannon-blast had rumbled away into the distance.

And only then did the man in the black fedora see and understand, accepted that he had failed at the very last. He ignored the cumbersome form of Don Devereux struggling up into a sitting position, switched his gaze back to that death-dealing cannon.

Haggard's pistol was aligned with the speed of a western gunfighter, the fingers of his left hand gripping his right gunwrist to steady it; picking a mark, it was not easy in the smoky firelight where flickering shapes came and went instantly. But he found the one he was seeking.

The gunshot went almost unnoticed amidst the screaming of the panic-stricken crowd. Haggard barely heard the report, felt the pistol buck in his grasp and saw his man spun round by the force of the striking bullet, thrown back against the ancient mortar, seemingly crucified on its ornate ironwork; then, finally, slumping to the ground, unheeded by those about him whose stampede for the exit places was barred by a line of police.

The man who called himself Haggard vaulted the barrier with ease and, still holding his .38 advanced on the sprawled, finely-clad actor whose white velvet jacket was spottled with crimson.

Tonight Death had called the roll, named his chosen and sent the fires of hell to claim the damned. Even Premier Kosminski and his entourage had not been spared the call.

CHAPTER TWENTY-TWO

Kosminski was back at the Katyn Memorial.

He had no idea how or why he was there, only that he was there. Landmarks were unrecognizable in the semi-darkness, the surrounding pines might have been trees in any wood, the soft springy grass a tract of heathland anywhere. He attempted to convince himself that he was somewhere else, far away from that terrible memorial to mass execution. Except that the stench of death which he had smelled earlier in the day seeped up through the soil beneath his bare feet, almost suffocated him with its vile putrefaction.

A dim awareness that he was clothed only in his silk lime green pyjamas, holding on to the trousers because the elastic was broken. There were people all around him, jostling him, silhouettes that reeked of the sweat of terror; faceless shapes that muttered incoherently, wrenching free of him when he grasped them, shouted at them in an attempt to make them listen.

Who are you? What is this place? Why are we here? Where is Orobin? And Kutuzov? Answer me or you will answer to General Jaruzelski?

No answer. Their touch was corpse-cold, their breath as foul as their body odours, milling around like cattle in a pen at the abattoir.

He shuffled with them, caught up in the awful tide, exhausted but there was no room to lie down, borne along with them until he lost all sense of direction. He tried to hold on to them but they pushed him away, buffeted him from one to another; he would have fallen had they not been bunched so tightly. All fourteen thousand of them! And if he fell they would trample him into the vile earth, tread him down beneath their wasted feet.

The pain in his chest was worse now. Anywhere else it would have frightened him, but here it was of no consequence, if you died then you joined the living dead in eternal torment. There was no escape.

They must have snatched him from his hotel bedroom whilst he slumbered restlessly, dragged him down deep into his own nightmares. His confused brain attempted to wrestle with logic. He had told Orobin that he was not going to the Festival; his bodyguard had come up with an alternative suggestion. Kosminski could not remember what it was, but evidently this was it.

It was a punishment, of course. Jaruzelski would have punished him for failing in his duty, and Orobin had acted in the general's absence. In Poland he would have been sent to Moscow for trial, transported secretly to one of the many camps.

And this was one of the labour camps.

Or perhaps they had drugged him, smuggled him back to *Katyn Forest.*

He tried to scream, managed only a strangled gasp of terror. He attempted to hold back, to bring this continual movement of shuffling inhumanity to a halt, but there were too many of them, they carried him with them. On and on, round and round in a never-ending circuit of the Pit. Dizziness threatened to engulf him; again he tried to hang on to them but they pushed him away, drove him on like a beast of burden.

He had been sent to Britain to be killed, he had no doubt about that. Then kill me, and have done with it! No, that was not the Soviet way, they wore you down, mentally and physically, reduced you to a zombie. There was no swift release from purgatory.

He did not know how much longer he could hold out, the pain in his chest was worsening, a constricting vice that was tightening all the time. If only he could find Orobin. His minder was a comfort to him in any situation, an invincible giant. Kosminski cried out for him again, tried to make faces out of shadows, peered at those who pushed past him, elbowed him roughly to one side. But they were all featureless silhouettes who reeked of death.

Except one.

The Polish premier saw him clearly where it was impossible to see, just as the other had seen through one-way glass from the opposite side. He recoiled, would have fallen but for the crush around him, was borne sideways so that he was compelled to gaze upon those features which he feared most, the pallid countenance that had haunted his waking and sleeping hours since his arrival in the city.

The stranger still wore that ridiculous wide-brimmed hat, tilted back now so that his face was clearly visible in the darkness; a kind of luminous glow seemed to emanate from it. Deep sunken eyes like glowing cinders, seething and hating. The thin lips were stretched wide, a ravenous wild beast which had run down its prey and was moving in for the kill, forcing his way through the moving throng, closing in.

'*No!*' Kosminski managed a cry this time, desperately trying to flee from his nemesis but there was no escape.

The man in black was alongside him, rubbing

shoulders with him, his closeness as cold as death itself.

'You didn't think you could escape by staying away from the Festival, did you, Premier Kosminski?'

Kosminski understood every word as clearly as if it had been spoken in his native tongue, a soft penetrating whisper borne on an Arctic wind, numbing him so that his reply was a series of inarticulate grunts; still being carried along, going somewhere, going nowhere.

'You're all finished, Kosminski,' there was a gloating in the other's voice now. 'Your corrupt regime has crumbled, is no more. Jaruzelski has gone, he can help you no longer. The tide of democracy has swept away communism as it has been threatening to do for a long time. Poland has formed a democratic government, the Berlin Wall has been taken down and is being sold as souvenirs. The peoples of the Eastern Bloc countries are free. All that has come about in your absence.'

'In . . . a . . . week?' Kosminski stared incredulously at the other. It was some kind of trick. A lie that was all part of his torture.

'You have been gone a lot longer than that,' the other spoke with a casualness that was a thousand times more terrifying than any hiss of malevolence. 'You're all going to die for the misery which you inflicted upon your fellow countrymen. There is no escape. Just as there was none that day in Katyn Forest. *Ask any of these people here, they'll tell you.*'

Suddenly the spectre in black was gone, vanished as if his ethereal glow had extinguished and condemned him to everlasting darkness with the rest of them. Kosminski clung on to a passer-by, defied the other's attempts to shake him off.

The man in the black fedora had spoken the truth,

strangely Kosminski did not doubt him. Jaruzelski and his puppet government had held on when it was obvious that their cause was a lost one. *Glasnost* had been an ever-widening crack, Solidarity an unstoppable foe. You could not subdue a nation by force forever. Communism, as he knew it, was a thing of the past, its perpetrators banished to this dreadful hell. Maybe Jaruzelski was here, too. If he was, then Kosminski did not want to see him; they had only one thing in common now, they were both wretched slaves to the oppressed in this stinking hell; they had ruled in life, now they served in death, their masters the living dead of Katyn Forest, Gdansk and other massacres.

Suddenly it was much warmer, a heat that was intensifying. Where Kosminski had shivered he now sweated profusely. A stench of burning assailed his nostrils, an acrid scorching that had his tortured lungs straining for air. The pace had slowed, somebody had fallen, the others stumbling as they trod their luckless companion down. He felt his feet on something that ballooned, writhed, gouged his leg with ragged fingernails. A cry of despair, it might have been a thousand miles away, the anguish of a doomed soul in torment.

Then came the flames, tongues of orange and yellow fire shooting up out of the earth, roasting the flesh on living bones, giving off choking fumes. An inferno, everybody fleeing but being forced back by an encircling wall of fire, a mound of corpses upon which the living dead scrambled, their blackened feet slipping in the melting fat. This, truly, was the domain of the terrible Antichrist.

Kosminski was back in his hotel bedroom, sitting up in bed, his fingers pressed against his palpitating chest; the electric light was painfully bright. Momentary relief because it had all been just another nightmare. Well, partly. He could still smell and taste the smoke from the incinerating corpses, the helpless screams of the still living dead echoed amidst the roaring in his ears.

The man in the black fedora had been a figment of his imagination, what he had said had all been lies; about the collapse of the communist regime and the spread of democracy. *That* could never happen, it was an impossibility. As impossible as the demolotion of the Berlin Wall. Or was it? There was no knowing the consequences of *glasnost*. Somehow the stranger's words had had a ring of truth to them. He would soon find out.

Where was Orobin? Of course, he had gone to the Festival along with Kutuzov and the others, a compromise following the premier's refusal to attend.

'All right, Premier, I will tell you what we will do. Give me your ceremonial uniform, our stature is similar. There will be no speeches to make. The platform, for security reasons, will be away from the glare of the floodlights. So who will know? Kosminski was there because we saw him, a distant shape surrounded by his entourage. Even General Jaruzelski will never know. What do you think, Premier?'

Good and faithful Orobin, always to be relied upon. Kosminski winced, cried out at the pain in his chest, a sensation akin to a knife being pushed into his breastbone. The nightmare was gone, this was reality and just as frightening. Death came in many forms, the end result was the same.

He cried out aloud, the effort sapping his waning strength. 'Help me, I am ill. *Don't let them take me back there!*'

But there was nobody out there on the landing to help him because nobody knew that Premier Kosminski was still in his hotel room. Right now he was on public view in the cathedral Close. And none would believe otherwise, they had no reason to.

Kosminski sank back on his pillows, the room was much darker now. He wheezed, struggled to breathe. Perhaps if he rested then the pain would go away and in the morning he would be on his way back to Poland. As soon as he landed in Warsaw he would demand that his physician visit him.

He started, tried to lift himself up, but his strength failed him. There was somebody standing just inside the door, a shadowy figure that was frighteningly familiar, only the brim of the fedora hiding those terrible features.

He could smell the smoke again, taste the burning human flesh. There was a roaring in his ears, the flames were scorching him, evaporating his perspiration. He gave up all thought of escape, resigned himself to his fate. He strained his smarting eyes but he was unable to see that fearful silhouette in the encroaching impenetrable blackness.

He heard the incessant tramping of feet, then the wasted bodies were jostling him again, taking him with them to wherever they were going.

Haggard stared down the barrel of a police pump-action 12-bore, elevated his eyes to meet those of the officer who held it, an authoritative, visored expression.

'Just lay that pistol down on the ground,' the policeman spoke calmly, trained to defuse an explosive situation. 'Nice and slowly.'

Rockets exploded over Stowe Pool like distant gunfire, a battle raging in the background. The giant bonfire crackled as it gained momentum, devouring the remnants of the huge platform less than a hundred yards away, its flickering glow seeming to bring to life the statues above the west doors of the cathedral. People were milling, screaming, and somewhere sirens were wailing, becoming louder by the second. Thick smoke billowed, brought with it the stench of burning corpses.

Haggard nodded, but only his free hand moved, held up something that glinted starkly in the smoky floodlighting, a square of white plastic. From a distance it might have been a credit card, anything. The policeman edged a step nearer to read it, and only when he had deciphered the lettering was his shotgun lowered. He stood back, did not enforce his command that this man in the black fedora lay down his .38 because, suddenly, he had no authority to do so. Neither surprise nor curiosity, just an impassive acceptance.

'Go ahead, sir,' he spoke with respect. 'If I can be of any help . . . '

'I'll let you know if you can.' Haggard moved past him, knelt beside the man who lay at the foot of the cannon, powdersmoke still wisping from its barrel. 'I think I can hear an ambulance on the way.'

'It'll be too late, not that I'm sorry.' Ron Borg coughed a dribble of blood, smiled weakly. 'You were just ten seconds too late. If you had me spotted, why didn't you . . . '

'Because I had figured it all wrong. I was watching the wrong man.' Out of the corner of his eye Haggard saw Don Devereux being helped to his feet, cursed the big man for what he was not. 'One thing I'll give you, Borg, you had me fooled right up to the last. By the way, I'm sorry about your son.'

'Don't be,' a touch of bitterness, 'he was no good, a wastrel. I just wish that he'd known that the Gospels he ruined were copies before he died. He wanted the Pole, too, you know, but he got side-tracked by his fanatical obsession with this animal liberation nonsense, and that was his downfall.' The gunsmith lapsed into silence, closed his eyes. The pain was worse now, the stain on his costume was spreading fast.

'Care to tell me about it. After all, you won the day. Gloat if you like. There isn't much time, we have to face it, you're not going to make it, Borg.'

Borg lay with his eyes closed. The ambulance was having difficulty in forcing its way through the crowds, the road was packed with people milling like cattle that had broken free of their pen at a livestock auction, going nowhere.

Haggard thought the other might be slipping into a coma but the eyes behind those rimless spectacles flickered open again. The one who had played the part of Sir John Gell, and had fired his home-made *grenado* with such devastating accuracy, spoke with a barely audible whisper so that the man in the black fedora had to lean close in order to hear. 'I guess I might as well, at least that way they'll know why. Otherwise, there's not much point, is there?'

It took the ambulance five minutes to gain entrance to the Close, by which time Ron Borg had finished talking. A doctor pronounced him dead before they lifted him on to the stretcher.

CHAPTER TWENTY-THREE

Chief Superintendent Clive Gardener felt damnably tired, there was no way he was going to get through another night without sleep. Miraculously, the tension, the threat of another panic attack, had receded. All he needed was his bed. He glanced at his watch, 3.20 a.m., looked back at the man sitting opposite him. Christ, what a night!

The Polish delegation had been blown up by a home-made cannon bomb, they were all dead, charred unrecognizable corpses; some unscheduled last minute switch by the Polish bodyguards, in an attempt to protect their premier, had proved futile. It had saved him from assassination, but not from death. Less than an hour ago a call had come through to inform the police that Premier Kosminski had been found dead in his hotel bedroom. A cardiac arrest, there was no suspicion of foul play.

The assassin in the Close had been shot by the man who had called himself Haggard. Now Haggard was gone, and with him the black fedora and the travel-stained dark clothing. A remarkable transformation that was in itself a tribute to the skill and tenacity of Sergeant John Mayo who had now replaced the character which he had created; a touch of sheer genius, the master stroke of a special agent. A portrayal that had bordered on the outrageous, Mayo's own camouflage to the point of ridicule.

Looking at Mayo now, dressed in casual clothing that did not accentuate the pallid complexion, Gardener thought that the other might have been a resurrection of Detective-Inspector Walters, or maybe any one of that faceless band of men whose job it was to protect national security; a similarity that became a nonentity, if you passed him in the street you would dismiss him at a glance, forget that you had ever seen him. He could barely remember what Walters had looked like, and when Mayo left the chief superintendent's only recollection of him would be that of Haggard. And Haggard would be as dead as Mayo's last assignment, created for a specific purpose and buried when the purpose had been served. One way or another, bar the shouting, it was all over.

Mayo did not have to explain to Gardener, he did not have to tell him a damned thing. That was up to the AC, but Mayo really liked the guy, felt sorry for him because all of this was outside the realms of the conventional copper, whatever his rank. But it had left its mark on the older man, etched a few more lines in his face. He had been to hell; fortunately, he had come back.

Pity was a rare luxury which Mayo decided to savour. It did you good once in a while. And, anyway, talking it through would help when he came to that part of the job he hated most, filing reports. If Wells was in a good mood he would allow his subordinate to dictate his report, have a secretary type it up. But Charlie wasn't likely to be delighted, there had been too many corpses left lying around, a messy finish. So Mayo had to get it right in his own mind, sort it all out in preparation for when the time came to get it down on paper. And this was as good a time as any, whilst it was still fresh in his mind.

'I figured to come in with this peace convoy,' he

spoke quietly but his words were clearly audible, 'and I had a hunch that this fellow Benjamin might lead me to the assassin. With hindsight, that hunch was right but the Antichrist angle blew it back in my face. I shot the guy to save a blaze which might have killed a score of people. Sure, this Benjamin was after the Pole but he had taken on too much, fell between all three of his stools. He got sidetracked by his obsession with animal rights. If anything, the proposed destruction of the Gospels was going to sidetrack him into trouble. I should have twigged the connection with the assassin when he boasted to me that he was going to join his father. I thought he was referring to his satanic master, but it was only later that I guessed the connection between himself and the assassin. He knew that his old man was going to have a crack at Kosminski and had decided that they stood a better chance if they joined forces. In fact, his father wanted nothing to do with him, but I guess Benjamin was hoping for a truce between them whilst they fixed Kosminski.

'Devereux was my man right from the time I arrived in the city. Which was where I slipped up, learned a few lessons that I thought I'd learned ten years ago. The chief was certain that we were up against The Wolf; that was bad enough but not half so bad as when Jean Bourgoin got himself shot in a London siege. That left us chasing shadows, and for me it was Devereux all the way. Devereux was French, he had an obsession with whores, and when that prostitute was found dead in the lake, I figured he was a dead cert, maybe even playing the Jack the Ripper game for kicks. Walters was on the wrong track, too. We did not collaborate, by the way. That way two agents can get on the wrong trail. Which we managed to do separately.

'Like I was saying, it wasn't Bourgoin from then on, and knowing Devereux's case history with call girls, I fell for the coincidence.'

'Borg murdered Sharon Vaughan, then?' Gardener asked.

'Yes. She was blackmailing him. He had been one of her clients for some time. He thought it a fitting twist, not only to silence her but to leave her as a Ripper-type victim to fuel the rumours that Kosminski was descended from the infamous Jack. God, Borg hated that Pole, but he would rather it had been General Jaruzelski himself, I'll warrant. Anyway, he decided to have a go at what was on offer, and if he succeeded then he'd look for a way to get Jaruzelski.'

'But why?'

'He married a Polish girl and they had a son, Benjamin. Anyway, as you know, there was a lot of unrest in Poland around the time Lech Walesa was arrested. Demonstrations were rife and Borg's wife joined one. The long and short of it is that the troops opened fire on a crowd of protestors and killed several. Borg's wife was one of the unlucky victims. Borg escaped to France, went back to his native Malta for a while, and then turned up in England. Benjamin did not manage to get out of Poland for a year or two, but when he did, he, too, came over here and discovered that his father was now a reputable Birmingham gunsmith. So we have a father and son both seeking revenge on those who instigated the killing of their respective wife and mother.'

'So Borg killed Walters, too?'

'Sure, but he was really cut up about that one. He had murdered the Vaughan girl without compunction, he had good reason to kill Kosminski, but he had no quarrel with Walters. Tim was a shrewd one. I think he was one move ahead of all of us and had tumbled to how the Pole was going to be assassinated. He must've gone to the Close to check on those cannons, looking for a *grenado*, and you only get careless once in this game. Borg knifed him, he had no choice, and from then on it was all or nothing, there was no turning back. Benjamin played his joker card, sprayed dye on the Gospels, and was convinced that he was invincible because he was the chosen one, the Antichrist. Like me, the cops were chasing shadows.'

'You can say that again!' Gardener puffed his cheeks. 'Tell me, did you really have to shoot Benjamin?' It was curiosity, not an accusation.

'Like I told you,' Mayo's gaze never wavered, 'it was either him or the folks down at the memorial. They would have been trapped in a wall of fire, the wind was right and the undergrowth was tinder-dry. I couldn't chance it. But I had a body on my hands then, and with an assassin in the vicinity, I didn't have the time to waste on explanations. I dumped Benjamin in that pool, hoped he wouldn't be found until it was all over. I just wish he'd known before he died that he'd wasted his time, sprayed black magic symbols all over copies instead of the originals. But, like his father, he died thinking he'd succeeded.'

'Do you think that . . . that there might be anything in this Antichrist business?'

Mayo shrugged. 'Depends on what you believe. But by now I was certain that Devereux was the man I was after. I checked out the first two probable assassination places, the Commonwealth Cemetery and the Katyn Memorial. There was nowhere right for a sniper in either, except for one place that I climbed up to, but I was damned sure that a man of Devereux's physique couldn't make it up there, let alone hide himself. It was all a process of elimination, two down and one to go. It *had* to be the Close. I was watching Devereux the whole time and I can promise you this, if it *had* been him then he'd've been lying under a shroud right now and the Poles would be still alive. But I made a mistake and it cost lives.'

Now it was Clive Gardener's turn to feel pity. Here was a man who had trained with the best fighting forces in the world, learned the Gurkhas' killing techniques, spent weeks hunting an unknown assassin, only to fall at the last hurdle. They would discipline him for his failure but you never heard about those kind of things. Perhaps John Mayo would find himself back on the open road for real before long.

'Borg had it all worked out, The Wolf himself couldn't have planned it or executed it better.' Mayo looked suddenly tired, an automaton that was running out of power. 'He had banked on Jaruzelski coming to Britain to reciprocate our own prime minster's visit to Poland some time ago, had planned accordingly and lived for that day. I guess his disappointment at it being Kosminski instead of the general was tempered by his unbelievable good fortune in that the Pole was coming to Lichfield for the Festival, literally walking into the lion's den.

'Borg was the obvious choice to organize the antique weapons for the mock siege. Again, fortune smiled on him. His chances of smuggling a modern weapon into the Close through the security checks were virtually non-existent but now he was actually in charge of weaponry, albeit obsolete, within killing range of his intended victim. The muskets were checked over by the police, but who would have bothered inspecting cannon and polystyrene cannonballs? So Borg made his *grenado*, matched it with the dummies, ensured that his cannon was trained on the VIPs' stand. You have to hand it to him for sheer cunning and marksmanship with a weapon that hadn't been fired for centuries. Bullseye! He blew 'em to smithereens, and even if I'd known it when he lay dying, I wouldn't have spoiled his finest hour by telling him that Kosminski had swapped places with one of his minders. But what's the difference, the bastard's dead and I guess that's all that matters to a lot of people. And I'd even go so far as to predict that these corrupt Eastern Bloc communist regimes are nearing the end of their day. Democracy is growing throughout eastern Europe and they won't be able to subdue it for much longer, you mark my words!' It was the first time that John Mayo had shown any emotion. It disappeared almost at once and he became the professional manhunter again.

'Did you *have* to shoot Borg? After all, he had fired his bomb, he wasn't a danger to anybody else.'

'Times like that, you don't take chances,' Mayo replied. 'Borg had committed two murders, now he'd blown up a foreign delegation. He could've had another *grenado* handy, gone kill crazy, done another Hungerford and gone for the crowd. I did what I was psyched up to do, what I'd've done if it had turned out to be Devereux. A mad dog has to be put down as quickly as possible.'

'I see.' Chief Superintendent Clive Gardener leaned back in his chair, closed his eyes briefly. The way Mayo put it, it made sense. Maybe others would see it differently, that was none of his business.

An embarrassed silence ensued, the kind that host and guest experience when conversation has run dry. Mayo was watching the other with an expression of expectancy, as though there was an inevitable question left unasked.

Gardener cleared his throat, began to doodle with a ballpoint on the jotter pad and when he spoke his eyes were firmly fixed upon the patterns he had drawn, began to ink them in. 'There's the girl, of course,' he said, 'we haven't mentioned her so far.'

'No,' Mayo averted his gaze, and for the first time there was a faint hint of embarrassment on his pale features, 'we haven't, have we?'

'We've been holding her for further questioning,' the chief superintendent felt himself swallow, a nervous schoolboy admitting some misdemeanour to his headmaster.

'She's in the clear,' Mayo spoke just a shade too quickly, 'you can take it from me. We travelled together on the convoy.'

'I know. She told me. We had to interrogate her, though, we didn't have any option. But she's free to go any time. She's in the interview room, third door on the left down the corridor.'

Mayo stood up, it was as though a heavy burden had been suddenly lifted from him. He smiled whimsically when Gardener said, 'You can just leave if you want to. She'll never know.'

The man who had been Haggard went outside and Clive Gardener sat there listening to the receding footfalls in the passage, shook his head slowly. These guys had no formula, there was no way of figuring them out. Which was why they were assigned to special duties. Damn it, he could not even remember what Mayo really looked like now that the fellow was gone.

CHAPTER TWENTY-FOUR

Penny sat in a confused silence in the empty interview room. She tried to understand, piece together scraps of information which she had gleaned from her interrogators. Haggard wasn't his real name, in a way that came as a disappointment. To her, he would always be Haggard, the man who wore the black fedora and carried a .38 Smith & Wesson in his rucksack. She didn't want him any other way. Now everything had spiralled to a climax, left her shaken and frightened.

John Mayo, they told her that was his real name, had used her for his own ends, she had been his link with Benjamin. Benjamin was dead and she was not sorry, just thinking about him had icy shivers trickling up her spine. The police said that Benjamin was the so-called Antichrist, a dangerous nutcase intent on destroying the Gospels. She tried to convince herself that he was no more than a madman, that that was where his evil terminated. The Polish delegation had been blown up with some sort of home-made bomb and the assassin was Benjamin's father. He was dead, too, shot by Mayo.

She told herself that she had to hate Mayo, that she had never really loved him. She had used him just as he had used her, a means by which to escape from Benjamin. Now it was all over. She fought to hold back her tears.

The police said she was free to leave, a WPC had

brought her a cup of coffee, it was cold and untouched on the table. She could walk right out of here, there was no reason to come back. Maybe she would go and crash out for a while at her parents' home, then try to find a new purpose in life. It would not be easy. Not after Haggard and all that he had meant to her. She wasn't going to be able to hold back those tears for much longer.

Suddenly she tensed as she heard footsteps in the corridor outside, recognized them instantly, that cat-like tread which would have been silent if there had been a reason for it to be. She sensed a weariness in the footfalls, mutely urged them to pass on by, recede into the street, become lost in the remnants of the Festival crowds. They didn't. They stopped right outside the door and she heard the knob beginning to turn.

No, *please*! I don't want to see you again. Ever. You've hurt me enough, just leave me to try to get over it.

The door opened slowly and she found herself staring at the man she had known as Haggard. Damn him, he still wore that black fedora as though to taunt her, his dark clothing dust-stained and dishevelled, his features starkly white in contrast. She tried not to meet his gaze but it was impossible.

'You okay?' He stepped into the room, kicked the door closed behind him and leaned up against it. He looked exhausted, mentally and physically drained.

'I'm all right.' Her voice quavered, any second she would cry.

'It's all over,' he said.

Yes, that was right, it was all over, there never had been anything between them, he had got what he wanted out of her, now he was going back whence he had come.

'We'd better go back to the hotel in the meantime.' His voice was strangely husky. 'Then maybe we can talk about where we go from here.'

Her heart flipped. It was another cruel trick, she wasn't going to fall for it this time. She opened her mouth to speak but the tears beat her to it. Then he was sitting on the bench alongside her, his arm around her, holding her to him and trying to kiss away her tears. She thought he might have been crying, too, but he was a good actor.

'You're a cop, then,' she said as soon as she was able to speak again.

'Of a sort.'

She gave up trying to hate him, let herself tremble in his arms.

'I had a job to do, I guess I blew it. But that doesn't alter anything between us. *If* you still want to tag along, that is.'

She stared up at him in disbelief, knew now that this was no trick, that he had meant everything all along. She nodded, still crying unashamedly.

'We'd better go,' he helped her unsteadily on to her feet. 'Police stations aren't the ideal settings for tearful reunions.'

Outside in the street the sky was clouded over, Penny thought she felt a rainspot hit her face. The long hot summer was over, the approaching storm would help to wash away the memories of the past few weeks, just leave her with the one she cherished most.

She glanced up at Mayo, trembled for a different reason now. She began to wonder what he was like in an ordinary lifestyle, where there was no place for a black fedora or a hidden pistol, where you cooked his meals and washed his clothes and did all those chores which hitherto she had regarded as boring and unnecessary. Suddenly, they had become an exciting prospect.

It began to rain heavily but neither of them cared. Right now they did not care about anything except each other.